StarWalker

Voices Crying to be Heard
Hope Trying to Emerge

A Novel by

Barry L. Callen

EMETH PRESS
www.emethpress.com

StarWalker
Voices Crying to be Heard
Hope Trying to Emerge
Copyright © 2011 Barry L. Callen
Printed in the United States of America on acid-free paper

Library of Congress Cataloging-in-Publication Data

Callen, Barry L.
 StarWalker : voices crying to be heard hope, trying to emerge : a novel / by Barry L. Callen.
      p. cm.
 ISBN 978-1-60947-021-0 (acid-free paper)
 I. Title.
 PS3603.A44624S73 2011
 813'.6--dc22
                                                        2011023983

Preface

Welcome to Lake Milton, and the little village of Craig Beach on its western shore. Don't misunderstand just because there is—at least was--a magical woods nearby that might remind one of the strange world of Jacob and Wilhelm Grimm. This village is a very real place between Akron and Youngstown, Ohio. Honest. In fact, it's been several places over the years, places that cover the entire history of the American people—and places with voices from yesterday still hoping to be heard and maybe even guide our tomorrows. Alright, I admit it. I do want you to be prepared. Not usually, but at least sometimes this village becomes a strange lazy Susan that turns quietly on an unseen axis and serves up other times and places. It happened fairly often for little Bud Kraemer. If you visit, just realize that it might happen for you too. Traveling the generations might make you dizzy and frustrated, or clear your brain and sharpen your eyes to the bigger picture of things. Either is very possible, and the choice to risk which it is entirely yours. What's evident to anyone who visits is that it's a small lake, about a mile wide at best and three or so miles long. Lovely as it is, it's artificial—real, mind you, but not really natural. That will be explained later. The village on its western shore is also small, some five-hundred permanent residents. But size isn't everything. Both lake with its marina and village with its amusement park are full of big significance—or so little Bud came to learn as the lazy Susan of the generations turned his way and he was willing to climb aboard.

Bud's learning came mostly from the mysterious StarWalker. Who he was, if he ever was and maybe still is, takes the whole story to explain. So let's get started with the tale. You have a personal invitation to both lake and village, to both other times and other places. As you read, please be careful. You might be vaulted into a yesterday you didn't intend, or maybe even be elevated into a different tomorrow you haven't thought of before. Again, that's your choice, your risk, your possibility.

If StarWalker befriends you, as he once did Bud, and you listen well, you'll know the right choice to make. Let's hope that secrets rooted back in World War II get revealed before everyone involved becomes a victim. Let's hope we can find the line between vision and delusion. Let's find a way to laugh before we all wind up crying.

So, let's go! Let's hope the old Indian shows up again—that is, if he ever did.

Chapter One

NOT MUCH LEFT

Finally, through the many hours of driving westward toward Ohio from eastern Pennsylvania, Bud Kraemer had managed to calm himself. He had been startled by what he had just learned.

One phone call can change the world! The fifteen years away from Craig Beach had eased the heaviness of his growing-up time back there, but those five minutes on the phone had dumped weight right on again. Bud had been away long enough that several things about him had changed. Just like his father, his hairline had begun to recede. Just like his mother, God bless her memory, a few extra pounds had gathered around his waist, although they didn't show as much on him because of his six-foot-two-inch frame. He had worn a modest beard since college days, a little attempt at independence and sophistication, but he decided to cut it off before he drove home. Some former classmates back at the lake might make fun of it, like they used to about nearly anything he did.

"That's stupid," he thought as he shaved quickly. "I'm a mature man now. I should get over such childish memories, painful as they are." But he hadn't, not entirely. Still, such memories dare not be allowed to get in his way. More important things had burst onto his agenda.

There was simply no choice now. After so many years, Bud had to go home, and fast. Once there, it would be straight to his father's side. Then, whenever he got a chance, he'd visit Morning Glen again. Maybe that place was just a bit of personal nostalgia for yesterdays long gone, but it was a spot in the woods near his boyhood home where the few wonderful memories he had of his younger life tended to linger. He'd take with him his walking stick. He didn't need a cane, of course, but he liked the security and looks of using that sturdy stick when in the woods. And it was really practical. He could place his wooden rod, like a friendly companion, across his shoulders and hang his arms on it if he got tired, or he could clear a cobweb ahead of him, or threaten an intruding dog. There also was a touch of British nobility in sporting the thing, even a little identification with what had once happened to Clarence, Abigail, and Joanna. It was right there in Morning Glen that he had heard about them from StarWalker, and about lots of other people too.

Bud fought against so many such memories washing over him. He had to concentrate on the one really important thing. His father was dying! The phone had rung so unexpectedly in his apartment. Within seconds of answering, Bud had found himself trying to comprehend what the news from Dr. Norton would mean for him. He had gotten himself packed, shaved, and on the road within hours.

On arrival in northeast Ohio the middle of the next day, he went quickly to his first stop, the nursing home in Pricetown, just two miles from his home of Craig Beach and where his old school was. What he found, as expected, was so sad.

Bert was lying there, his tall and wide frame now looking shrunken by several inches. His skin was a little leather like, the natural result of his rugged work over the years and his time at sea before that. His eyes were closed tightly, almost like he was hoping to deny the presence of the various things now hooked to his aged body. No communication was possible, at least not yet. The nurse said he'd not be awake for hours, the result of medication they'd given him. There was nothing to do except stare at him for a few minutes, hold his cold hands, and then leave and come back later.

So, out to the parking lot he went, back the two miles to Craig Beach, down Beach Lane past the little house where he had grown up, and on the two more blocks to the edge of the woods. While he thought he could find some solace in Morning Glen, the little clearing a short distance into the woods, he was immediately shook up yet again. "It's too much—and not fair!" The tip of his stick must have startled that little snake, maybe even nicked it by accident. Thinking its world was about to end, it had slithered away in a streak of green desperation, causing Bud's heart to skip a beat or two.

"My poor ticker doesn't need that right now!" Bud looked at his shaking hands and had to admit to himself that he was actually afraid.

What if, instead of retreating, the snake had attacked him, sinking fangs into his leg before he could move? But he couldn't think only of himself. "I don't know whether snakes have hearts. If they do, this little one must have been racing wildly too. We really scared each other!" The last thing Bud needed right now was venom in his veins. He wasn't ready for his father and himself both to go to the great beyond. He took several deep breaths, quieting himself in the good, clean air of the woods. No damage had been done—the snake was out of sight, an emergency over as fast as it had begun.

"We sure are a pathetic pair!" It was unbelievable. Not the presence of the snake. They were common and not dangerous, at least so Bud's parents had told him when he was a kid. There weren't that many snakes, not around this village in northeast Ohio, especially not this far away from the lake. Does danger always increase as water nears? Maybe. Whatever the truth, Bud recalled that some of his boyhood around this lake had been pleasant, fang free; but lots of it hadn't been. That was a long time ago, yet lots of questions from those days remained unanswered.

What was really surprising was his being back to the lake and village, and now even back in his little wooded hideaway after so many years. It didn't appear to have changed much, just a new shift of leaves on their same old rounds of limb to ground, and a new generation of snakes no braver than before. But he certainly had changed.

"I'm no longer a struggling little kid, the butt of bullies, fearful on the school bus and worried about Mom and Dad at home—they did have their problems." He was embarrassed, mumbling to himself like an emotional kid when now he was an educated teacher barely literate when back in the old woods. Bud had to face it. He was still wounded and wanting comfort from any source. He had found some in this secluded spot many times, but that was many years ago.

Bud felt like an overly mature leaf ready to fall, a silly snake about the panic, a weakening old tree terribly afraid of the next big wind, a little boy in a man's body humbled and confused in the face of his dad's impending death. At least it was easier to think out here in the woods. It always had been, which is why it was so important to come again at a difficult time like this. Bud surely had lots of thinking to do.

He let his bottom land gently on a clump of grass more moist than he had expected. He admitted to himself that he was hiding from the harsh reality in the nursing home, longing for isolation from life's pressing problems. Once he had been a star-gazing and village-romping little boy; now, here he was using a strong walking stick, about to jump at his own shadow if something moved. He didn't really need the stick, of course. Oh well, it seemed to guarantee good balance on uneven ground, the very ground that he once knew so well and passed over with such ease.

He was gripped by a sad thought. "I suppose Dad will be under some ground like this pretty soon."

And what about his old friend who used to meet him here in the woods and carry him off to magical, mythical, maybe even real places of long ago? That Indian must have been ancient when Bud once knew him. Still, he had seemed ageless.

"I suppose that somehow he's still alive, at least in his own way, or at least in my memory, maneuvering out there somewhere, talking to other boys, still trying to make the world right. He was a great old guy!"

They say there's a fine line between a genius prophet speaking about tomorrow and a crazed idiot not in touch with the simplest sparks of reality. StarWalker—that was the old Indian's name--had at least seemed to be more the former. A man, however, can't be sure about such a strange thing, especially when stressed and inclined to extremes.

"How silly, even ridiculous," Bud thought. He was a mature man now, out in the woods recalling what might have been only boyhood delusions, even talking to a snake that already was out of sight and could care less about his problems. Was he losing it? He did it anyway, just kept talking to himself.

"I'm so sorry, little snake wherever you are, but you scared me too!" With that off his conscience, he did some more serious reflecting. Bud used to come to this very spot to get over being scared and confused; now he'd come back and thrown fright into a little creature, and was trying without much success to apologize to an absent reptile without ears.

"Please relax wherever you are. Look, little snake, I'm putting down my dangerous stick, right on the bare spot where StarWalker and I used to sit with our legs crossed, Indian style, and have our amazing little talks."

Bud hadn't been home for a long time. The village of Craig Beach was home, at least it used to be. He had to come back this time given the heavy news from that phone call. And now, barely back, he was already talking nonsense in nature! So what if the snake wasn't about to reappear. Maybe StarWalker would—well, no, not likely, not to an older man. Maybe the ancient Indian was the eternal voice of wisdom that spoke only to young boys and girls who still have ears to hear such things. Or maybe he never had been there in the first place. Troubling "maybes"!

They also say that there's a fine line between the marvelously real and the merely magical, what actually is and the unreal that gets dredged into consciousness by an overactive imagination. A lot had happened that led to Bud's leaving home in the first place. The reason for his finally coming back was sad, very sad, but there was no real choice. If only he wouldn't mess up everything, first the snake and then his dad. It had been way too messed up around here before!

Some of those old things had to be rethought now that he knew the contents of those surprising letters in his mom's little treasure chest, and the bank key too, of course. They sure made things appear a lot different than he had understood them when he was a boy. Hopefully there was time left to make things right with his dad before death slammed the door shut forever.

As he'd been traveling back, Bud had brought with him the wounds of his years, most dating back to his younger days. Some of them were visible, like the little scar on the side of his neck and that splotchy reddish burn mark on the back of his left hand. They were emblems of difficult yesterdays for himself and his country. Each emblem had a long story of its own.

Today, however, wasn't the time for these stories. Crowding to the front of the line was the fresher scar inside, a big pain in his heart, a surge of love badly wanting to get out and start some healing--if it could, if enough time was left.

Dr. Norton had told him on the phone that his dad was dying. Hearing that, Bud knew instantly that he at least had to try to do what he knew had to be done. Now back in the village, he hadn't made much progress, only a first stop at the nursing home that yielded no conversation because of his dad's drugged sleep. Then, after scaring the snake and dribbling a half-meant apology out his mouth, he had sat on his beloved spot of bare ground in the woods wondering about old StarWalker. It was embarrassing to have to wonder if he could manage to get back up without help if he crossed his legs too long! Does a little time do that to everybody?

Bert had been living alone in the same old place, at least before this nursing home business had jerked him up by the roots. In recent years, he hadn't seemed to care about much of anything, even living. That's what Dr. Norton had said. Bud was Bert's only child, and now maybe his only lifeline left. He clutched tightly the little treasure chest of his mother's that he had brought with him. If only years ago he'd read those letters in it. He had no idea his dad had written them during the war or ever had feelings anything like what they documented so graphically. Well, he knew now.

"How could I grow up and know so little about who my parents really were? They must have hidden themselves from me deliberately. But why, why? Man! I really didn't know my dad at all, and now I'm all that's left for him—and I have so much I want to tell him. Truth is, I'm barely hanging on by a thread myself. I'm so full of doubts and hopes, regrets and new insights about my dad and mom, and I don't know what to do with them."

Bert certainly was in no shape to help. Bud would have to hang on and be strong for both of them. His mysterious friend in the magical woods years ago had made the difference for him on many critical occasions—showing up with friendship and wisdom. If only time now would allow the son to make a difference for his dad!

Bud's head had been full of these sober memories and anxious thoughts long before he got to the nursing home and to this wooded clearing on the edge of the village of Craig Beach. They had filled his very being as he drove through the Mahoning Valley of northeast Ohio, including right through Youngstown on his way home. A big percentage of the steel used by the United States to win World War II had been produced in this immediate area—a matter of considerable pride to the locals. But now that same steel industry had shed nearly ninety percent of its former work force.

At their peak, those fiery furnaces had unleashed hell with its lid clear off. With the lid now tightly back on, the place felt as cold as a buried casket in Siberia. There was so much decay to see. As the weight of this cultural sickness bore down on him, Bud had grieved as he drove and looked. The grief was for the place, but more for his father who earlier had been so much a part of this place and all it stood for.

Bud's thoughts were somber, verging on the morbid. "Maybe industries, maybe nations, apparently even people have their birth-death cycles. They seem to flourish and then wither, run their courses, have their big days in the sun and then just fall apart. How awful!" That was now his dad's experience. His strength was withering away toward death, pride smashed to the ground, a roaring fire of sturdy manhood about to be extinguished.

Bud had steered and stared, his hands tightly holding the wheel, his white knuckles showing his inadvertent revulsion caused by the passing sights. He saw one old steel plant with weeds growing two feet high in the cracks of the parking lot. A sagging roof looked as if any reasonable wind could finish it off. Someone had spray-painted a pathetic message on a block wall that was partly gone. It read, in rough-shaped and dripping letters: "They took the heart out of me when they shut these mills. I didn't mind the dirt. It was bread on the table!"

That sorry sign brought on a little prayer that Bud had mumbled as he drove along—he was just beginning to deal with this God thing, not by going to church, at least not yet, but by testing little prayers when in trouble and no one else was around to hear. Some of his language was biblical, some absorbed from StarWalker, the old Indian of yesterday's Morning Glen.

"Dear God, or Great Spirit, or whoever you are, keep me from collapsing into depression like the rest of this place. Help me comfort my dad and apologize to him and finally tell him I love him. Maybe Dad's the one who painted that miserable message on the wall. Who knows? What a terrible thought! Help me to paint a very different message for him on the sides of his soul, or what's left of it. And, for sure, help me get there in time."

The sickness of radical social change had happened in the Youngstown area in the late 1970s and early 1980s while Bud was far away building another life. Steel once had been king; now it was pauper, leaving men like Bert Kraemer in the dust of an empty factory, in the rust of abandoned machinery, in the dying bodies and decaying souls of men who once had made it all work so well that they had saved the world from evil dictators. But that was another time, a hideous Hitler time, a stimulating time of meaningful work and massive production. This time was so different. The rest of Bert's story was in those letters only recently read by Bud, with their shock still fresh for him. At least he thought it was all there.

"I'm coming home, Dad. Wait for me! I'll try to shake off these sad sights and thoughts and be a carrier of some hope."

Suddenly, he remembered why he had his own first name. According to what his mom once told him, "Bud" was chosen because he had been the fresh-flower little boy for her, a new springtime gift from God, the one bright spot in her life. That's exactly what Jessica had said to her little son, God rest her soul. He knew that, at best, he now would be able to spread only a little if any fragrance of hope to help his dad, that is, if he could keep himself together, be the brave flower of a new day and not just another flake of decay falling off an old something or other from former days of glory. It wouldn't be easy with all of his own scars, inside and outside, and his dad's very poor health and deep depression. Important things often aren't easy.

"Why does it have to be this way? No matter. These are the days I have and during which I must try!"

It probably was a little boyish for Bud, no longer a kid, never married, and now in his middle thirties. Maybe it was nothing but a wave of silly nostalgia, but Bud had to know. Was everything changed? So, as soon as he had visited his father for that first time, spending an hour in that depressing nursing home, with Bert having said nothing and not even moving the whole time, and the smell of the place making a visitor feel suddenly old himself, Bud had driven to the west side of Lake Milton. He passed the now-bare ground where the amusement park once was, and went on down Beach Lane. The goal was to glimpse the little house of his boyhood and then go the three more blocks to the edge of the woods. That's when and where he had startled the poor little snake. The house was there, although looking smaller and shabbier than he remembered it.

What about the wonderful woods? Do trees also shrink over time? Does everything collapse, corrode, get drugged, curl up and die, leaving nothing of value behind? He had to find out!

Chapter Two

OLD RADIO WAVES

O ne of Bud's favorite radio programs had been on in the car as he had driven through Youngstown. That mellow and measured and yet hilarious voice gave a little relief from the sad scenes outside. The program had so filled him with emotion that he could hardly contain it. Garrison Keillor's *A Prairie Home Companion* show had been joking along, amusing Bud. Then he realized that there were tears in his eyes, partly from laughing and partly from the sheer weight of nostalgia. It was ignited by Keillor's memories of that fictitious little place in Minnesota called Lake Wobegon.

"It's not on the maps," Keillor was saying, "but only because incompetent surveyors in the nineteenth century had just missed it!" That made Bud giggle out loud—fortunately there was no one else to hear his slightly out-of-control silliness. And looking outside the car, it obviously wasn't humor time anyway. He spoke to himself, drowning out Keillor's continuing monologue.

"Steelworkers are outdated these days, and surveyors were so stupid in those days!" Lake Wobegon never was, of course, and this steel city hardly was anymore. Who beyond this immediate area has even heard of

Craig Beach, real as it is? Oh, well, it was home for Bud and he was coming back, at least for a few days.

Keillor had more to say—and was being heard again as soon as Bud stopped his own talking. "When a boy in that no-place Minnesota town that had been missed, I had used a secret place under the stairs of my home to read and write. And there also had been a little ravine, a dry creek-bed on the edge of town where some friends and I hid away to share secrets and tell boyish tales that we never would have breathed aloud at home."

That Minnesota memory began swirling around in Bud's ears, head, and especially heart. He hoped he would not be disappointed when he got to his home village. He had his own version of a ravine locked in his memory and heart—there were no stairs in the little house in Craig Beach where he grew up. The Kraemer family was lucky to have had the small place they did.

After that first and frustrating visit to his dad's room, and with Keillor now silenced in the car, Bud had reached the second goal of his journey, his own under-the-stairs and down-in-the-ravine secret place where as a boy he had felt free, in touch, safe, almost wise. He hadn't gone there with friends since usually they were the source of his problem—especially Mike Jakas. Bud had parked his car at the end of Beach Lane, back in Craig Beach village, on the western shore of Lake Milton. He then had walked into the woods, hoping to find again that other world that used to be his alone. It wasn't on the map—they had missed this place too!

The tangle of trees was still here. Simple as it was, it was strangely comforting, even exciting, like being really home again. Bud had filled with memories as he cautiously wandered off the road and into his fantasyland. That was just before the sudden snake scare. "I'm so glad that time doesn't take everything away!"

To be more exact, it wasn't the woods in general calling to him, but that old, memorable, even magical clearing in the woods. That's what Bud really wanted to see again, feel again, maybe even be enlightened by again. And sure enough, only a short walk from the car, there it was, still nestled among the same old trees. It wasn't anything, not really. Still, it was his sacred, secret, boyhood hideaway place—and to him that was really something.

Even though there was nothing there but bushes, brush, and broken limbs that the aging trees had let tumble to their tired feet, there still were other worlds for Bud that only he could see, feel, imagine, and anxiously cherish. They always had been there for him, or at least since the first time StarWalker had appeared in this very place and opened the books of the past so that a boy could see into himself, and into yesterdays, and even into tomorrows still to come.

It was true. Wild worlds once swirled in this very clearing. The Iroquois had been on the warpath against the Erie Indians—right here! The British regulars once were charging with fire in their eyes, and colonial homes were about to be set ablaze—right here! Yes, not two miles from this very spot, Fredericksburg once was grabbing its last breath as the flood was about to swallow it into the pit of dark-liquid oblivion. A whole town had died—right here!

He'd lived it all before, right in this little clearing, and Bud the boy had learned a lot. Being here again and remembering all of this was both scary and healing, frightening and settling, confusing and yet the source of rare wisdom. Such mixtures of apparent opposites were part of the magic of the place, the complex way life really is. This day, though, the clearing was strangely quiet. Maybe all that was once there for Bud had already died and was snuggled somewhere under the leaves, probably rotted away long ago.

Bud's thoughts were full of disappointment. "No one else is here, or likely cares to be, or knows the place exists and even has a name. It's *Morning Glen.* At least it used to be called that by StarWalker and me. Maybe now it's a place of mostly shadows rather than sunrises. Maybe it's given in to the crashing society just beyond its borders."

The clearing was the definition of nowhere, at least in the dictionary of the uninitiated. But Bud belonged. He knew, he could see, he remembered, and he was back in search of more help. He was laboring, now feeling like one of the older trees hanging on to the few leaves still left on its branches, wanting to look up, way up, pleading for lostness in the distant sky, release from agony, hoping for the returning presence of an old friend who knew so very much. Maybe by now the Indian's time had ended and he was entombed under something nearby.

Bud got himself comfortable and looked longingly upward for several meaningless minutes, eyes and imagination straining, wishing he could see the old man one more time. That ancient Indian had come to him before, right here, and always just in time. His past appearances had been either real, and thus wonderful beyond description, or imaginary and pathetically delusional and disappointing in the extreme. People say there's little distance between genius and insanity. Bud was ready to settle for just a little normality, a touch of stability if any were to be had for himself and his dad.

The old man had called himself StarWalker. He'd been such a friend, a wise guide into life's bigger mysteries, a light to help a young man see how to build a life in deeply troubled days. That ancient one had walked among the stars in the sky, so he said at least, crossed the fleeting generations, knew of the many days gone by, and he had been willing to show a boy the paths to better living. That was years ago, of course, the old Indian stuff, but what about today?

It remained quiet in the clearing, empty of evident meaning and activity except for a squirrel that bolted in the leaves, startled by this strange visitor who randomly tossed a stone in frustration. Was there any creature not frightened by Bud's presence? Was he intruding? Did he not belong anymore? He was so alone, except for the squirrel, and that hiding snake, and the memories that swirled within him about so much now apparently buried beneath the leaves. And his dad added to the aloneness. He hadn't moved or made a sound on that visit to the nursing home. There also was no StarWalker, not today, maybe never again--maybe there never was.

Do people finally outgrow their taste for mystery, their openness to the eternal, their sensitivity to the spiritual? The wonder of boyhood easily succumbs over time to the deadening dust and decaying rust of the years—like those sad steel plants around Youngstown. And yet, Bud also was tiring of the nothingness of doubt and cynicism that were his life. He had begun testing at least the edges of faith—even risking a little prayer now and then, not sure if he should expect any kind of response.

Had he lost eyes that could see beyond the moment? If so, how could he possibly be of any use to his dad? It turned out that his dad was lovable, even wonderful, despite the past. Bud hadn't ever thought of Bert in such an intimate way before, not until finally opening that chest and reading those letters. And now it may be too late to share with him his new feelings. Then came a frightening thought.

"Maybe I'm now StarWalker! Maybe the mantle has fallen on me to be the link of wisdom between yesterday and tomorrow, a link for some boy or girl, even for one dying old man!" But this possible Indian substitute wasn't sure he had any wisdom, and hardly knew any really young people, certainly not around here, and he didn't have a wife or any kids of his own. Come to think of it, the marks on his body were much the same as those he remembered on the old Indian. Was that just a coincidence, the little neck scar and the burn-like mark on his left hand? There were lots of unanswered questions like that.

"Does the student finally become the teacher? Could a middle-aged man bring any joy, any hope or wisdom to a despairing father whose days were about done and whose very world was on its last legs? Does yesterday really help us know anything important about tomorrow? Don't times become really different, so that the old 'A' doesn't fit the new 'B'? Don't most of us just forget anyway? Sure we do, but do we have to? Can we afford to? Is there any choice?"

Enough of that for now. Bud's eyes had been closed as he was searching for answers that hadn't come. Now he let them open slowly and absorb the bright sunlight breaking through the trees. Spinning in mental circles can get a guy only one place, dizzy and nowhere. He needed to stop dreaming and check on his father again.

Out of the clearing and back to the car, Bud returned up Beach Lane, past the old house of his boyhood—it really did look smaller than he remembered, and then by the amusement park that was no more. Next came Sinclair's grocery store that had a new sign over the door— whatever happened to the fascinating Mr. Sinclair? Bud went around Lake Milton on its north side and back to the nursing home to visit again the leftovers of a once proud man.

This was Bud's somber itinerary, a short two miles from the fleeting inspiration of his old hiding place to today's nursing place, from the security of a lost past to the despair of a desperate present. He passed the dam that had created this lovely lake in the first place, and then he saw the old school of his boyhood in Pricetown, a crossroads of about forty scattered residents. Finally, there it was again, that sterile-looking brick building housing the still-living remains of Bert Kraemer.

It had to be faced. There wasn't much of value left of former days. A culture once so alive and dominant was now in decay, a shadow of its former self. The earlier guide to the truths of the ages seemed to be no more—the stars were still there, but not the voice of wisdom that once walked among them, appeared to a little boy, and explained their mysterious meanings. Twinkling tiny lights, when without an interpreter, are no more than a jumble of faint voices, each speaking an unknown language to ears that can't escape their own deafness. Life itself seemed to be slipping away for the dad, and wallowing in the mud of meaninglessness for the son.

Bud mumbled aloud in the car as he drove back into the parking lot. "Not much left, that's for sure." Maybe that snake and squirrel were the lucky ones. They just act on instinct, with no disturbing memories of yesterday and no anxieties about envisioned tomorrows that may never be. They just function thoughtlessly, fear for nothing except a little famine or a sudden fox or dog--or big man with a walking stick! They have no concern for loss of meaning, no desire for perspective beyond the moment.

Safety, food, and reproduction are the only agenda items of their lives, nothing to do but play, eat, duck when necessary, and find a nice mate. What a desirable way to live!

"Dear God," Bud breathed quietly before he opened the car door. "Either lower me to a dumb but fulfilled animal or fill my vacant soul with something that satisfies, and please help me to do the same for my dying dad." Then, instead of getting out immediately, he leaned on the wheel and allowed his mind to run loose with a stream of thoughts.

Maybe his writing would help—if not help his dad, maybe others who'd never even been to northeast Ohio and the little spots in it like Pricetown and Craig Beach village. Like Keillor on the radio, Bud had done a little writing of his own, first in the secret clearing, and much later as a man trying to make sense out of a changed world far from Lake Milton. He now was a teacher, an educated man of literature, a searcher spending time with the mature thoughts of others and trying to get teenagers interested in reading and thinking.

Bud had not forgotten something a teacher once told him—her name had been Miss Mason and she had taught right here in Pricetown when he was a boy (could she still be there?). Looking out the schoolhouse window at the nearby cemetery, she had asked Bud, "Who out there isn't dead?" It was a strange question with no apparent answer. This teacher was serious and finally ended Bud's puzzlement with this: "Only those who wrote!" She was encouraging Bud to think deeply, focus his thoughts, and put them on paper so that they could stay alive. He had tried to respect her advice over the years. Still, he knew nobody was likely to read his work. If not, the process of writing had helped him think, so it would have been worth it.

There also hung around in his memory something he'd heard on the radio as he'd recently driven through Youngstown. A country woman had once said some things about rhubarb to Garrison Keillor at a fair where he was broadcasting on the radio.

"How silly." Bud scolded himself. "I'm facing Dad's death and my inability to tell him important news first, and here I am pondering the lovable qualities of rhubarb!" He continued remembering what he'd heard while sitting with his hands still gripping the wheel of a car that hardly needed to be steered since it was sitting motionless in the parking lot.

"It's not something widely available commercially—not much market for stuff most people don't want." Apparently rhubarb was a popular dessert in Lake Wobegon, a hit at fairs, a local delicacy in Minnesota, but rarely in Ohio, at least as far as Bud could remember.

The woman had gotten downright philosophical about rhubarb, announcing that it's a good metaphor for finding happiness in your own backyard (where most of it is grown). Yes, it is a green, leafy, rather sour metaphor. So what? Keillor himself had come from country people with such backyards, and his radio show celebrated the simple stories of life in his own boyhood town. Bud now wanted to do the same. There were memories to celebrate about lots of people he'd once known around here. But that didn't look likely, not now anyway.

He'd learned over the years that most people seem to get their political and religious ideas from listening to others rant and rave on some public medium--which he'd never heard Keillor do, but which used to happen regularly at the local bingo night when he was a kid. Bingo became the social center of the village world, especially after the amusement park closed. The ranting and raving usually was (is?) based on personal preference, private prejudice, and unchecked emotions overcoming reason and ignoring actual information. That left Bud with lots of questions.

"Isn't that relatively mindless process true of religion as well as politics? Wasn't it Shakespeare who once wrote that our lives are so much sound and fury, and they turn out to signify nothing much when we finally quit breathing?" That literate old Englishman had written the question and shared the cynicism. Miss Mason had been right. Because of the writing, the bard's thoughts were still alive, disturbingly alive, just like Bud's thoughts were supposed to be if he didn't forget to write them down.

He could almost hear Miss Mason making little speeches in English literature class back in high school. She once said that there was another writer, Thomas Hardy, who had written lines that stuck in his memory, lines hardly comforting to him right now.

> The dreaming, dark, dumb Thing
> That turns the handle of the idle Show.

It was time to grab the handle and get out of the car. After a few nervous steps, Bud was staring at the door he needed to go through again.

Would his dad still be breathing? Was that it, all of it? Was that all there is to life? Breathe for a few years and then just quit and that's it? Sure, there's a little dreaming when you're young, but then comes the darkness, the dumbness, the turning and turning by something that ends up being nothing? Then came another prayer to Bud's quivering lips.

"Dear God! If you're there, and if Hardy's wrong, can't you please speak up? I need to hear you! Dad needs to hear you, too."

Such sober thoughts and literary fragments and pieces of painful prayers made Bud wonder about the sources of his own ideas. Had those fascinating stories told by StarWalker in the secret clearing only been so much nothing, the delusions of a little boy, the dreams of an old man who never was? Is there enduring meaning in such sacred memories, or are they only a murky mist, made up and dead-end stuff, best forgotten if a guy can manage it? Was the end here for Bert, for Bud's own past, for everything related to anything of any lasting meaning? At least a son had come home to his father and wanted to try—try something that could make the end just a little better for both of them.

A thought shot across Bud's mind. "Oh, to be a mere snake in the grass or a squirrel on the run!" But no such luck. Reality had to be faced and some things had to be shared with Bert Kraemer—unless, of course, it was too late.

Chapter Three

SECRET PLACES

It hadn't always been sad around Lake Milton. Far from it! Bud's family had come to the village of Craig Beach on the lake's western shore soon after the big war was over—although an armed guard remained on duty at the dam every day and night to protect Youngstown's steel industry. That water was a vital reserve. It was time to get on with life. Sure, sometimes getting on had to happen for many war veterans in out-of- the-way places like Craig Beach. Housing and money were scarce. Still, the world was at peace and life had a chance to get going again.

The lonely little clearing in the woods was just down Beach Lane, barely three blocks from where Jessica and Bert Kraemer had first come to live. Hitler was dead and Japan had been subdued. That generation of Americans, later to be called "the greatest," had saved the world from dictators and disaster, and now it had to move on in less dramatic but still demanding circumstances. Craig Beach was a modest but affordable little place to try getting on with things.

Back then, and despite no sidewalks in the village, it was an easy walk to about anywhere. One way from the Kraemer house led to the woods; the opposite direction took one to the amusement park which sat very near the lake. It was a privately owned fun place with a dance hall, bowling alley, and children's rides—not to mention food concessions for the indulgent and a palm reader for the offbeat. On crowded summer evenings, you had to be careful turning your head suddenly or you might come uncomfortably close to sharing someone else's hot dog, all bloodied on the end and sticking out in your direction. The crowds were happy, spending whatever they had on their every whim. If weekdays were drudgery in Youngstown's mills, the weekends would try to make up for it.

Bud was the only young Kraemer and, one would think, he lived in the perfect place for a boy. On magical evenings, the music from the merry-go-round at the amusement park would drift up Beach Lane until nearly midnight. It would join the warm night air in coming through the window screen right into the little bedroom of Bud. The playful notes of the merry-go-round were repetitive, joyful, almost hypnotic, at least on the surface. Actually, they were artificial, coming from a machine hidden in the middle of the circled horses made of wood, painted in gaudy colors, and bolted to the moving platform so they couldn't escape. Amusement was the purpose of the little park, about the only life-blood of the village in the summertime, except for the lake itself, of course.

Boating, fishing, and water sports of all kinds were the local way of life. For Bud, however, things were mostly dull; the music helped a little, although he knew that it had more splash than depth, and most things in the park cost money. An only child in a home of modest means and personal preoccupations, to say the least, he had to amuse himself most of the time—or just exist in his private world of growing anxieties.

The music would go on and on while the imitation horses went up and down, round and round, on some days hardly stopping on their pointless circular journeys to nowhere. The horses were mounted on posts that moved up and down, driven by gears designed to simulate a galloping motion. The horses had handles screwed to them. The children could cling to them while they took their paid-for journeys of make-believe joy. The day would come when a "carousel" would be a big area in an airport where hundreds of suitcases would go in circles, hoping to be claimed by owners after flights from somewhere to somewhere else, a loud and often frustrating place of found and lost luggage. What Bud knew, however, was the one in Craig Beach. It was colorful, musical, delightful, going from nowhere to nowhere, with the fun in the journey itself. All too soon the entire park would be gone, but not while Bud was growing up.

Kids like Bud had a tendency, if not watched closely, to jump on and off while the carousel was still in motion, loving the whole thing, and upsetting the operator whose job it was to collect quarters for each ride and keep people from getting hurt. But to the frolicking kids going in circles, it was really fun, not the pointless stupidity some parents thought. To Delores and Shirley and John, young people of the village and class-mates of Bud, working in the park at various odd jobs meant some diver-sion and pocket money.

Things would go a little wrong sometimes. A few kids finally would get dizzy and have to get off before ruining their clothes with the half-digested junk food they had talked parents or grandparents into buying for them right before the ride. Fun isn't always free or healthy. It isn't necessarily even rational. And in Craig Beach, it had to be summertime for any fun to be available in the park.

When winter came, the park was locked and its entrances fenced. The village became low-key at best. There was a local fire station about six blocks away from the park, but it also remained locked unless there was an emergency. When there was, a horn would blow from its roof and vo-lunteers who happened to be at home would hurry to open the place and see if the old truck would start and had any water in it—no fireplugs meant that water had to be hauled to the trouble spot. It was definitely better if fires didn't start in the first place! It also was a good idea to keep a close eye on kids. They often played on the lake in the dead of winter if the ice was thick enough—the problem was that you could never be sure and might soon be dead if you took the risk and were unlucky. But there were always those who relished the risk. Bud wasn't among them. He was one the timid side and wasn't about to violate the orders of his fa-ther. He was to stay off that lake in the winter.

Bert was only twenty-four when he first arrived in the village with Jessica and little Bud. His life to that point had seen only two places, northeast Ohio and the Pacific theater of war. That was already one too many places for him. He was slender, strong, independent, now a smok-er, something Jessica disliked, but tolerated. The Kraemers didn't have much, but at least he was home, still breathing, with all limbs attached, and they had each other and hope, always hope.

They talked almost every day about how they were going to get along now that the war was over and the peace had to be survived as well as enjoyed. They were glad for the chance, hard as it would be. Bert's typi-cal comment to his young bride was sober, but determined.

"Well, Jess, this little village isn't much, and Beach Lane's hardly an avenue to anywhere important, unless you count the little park midway and the beach just beyond, but it's a lot better than that Midway island place out in the Pacific. The music down the street might only be seasonal and cheap entertainment, but at least it's harmless and pleasant sounding. And the little kiosk between the merry-go-round and the beach sells French fries doused in vinegar that have got to be the best anywhere 'round. They'll fill up my frame a little if I don't stay clear of them!"

Jessica agreed. "They sure are good, and you know, my dear, I'll do all I can to make this little dump of a summer cottage into a home. If Ike's made it to the White House in D. C., and the French fries don't run out, we can make it too."

"Yea, Ike's quite the story, Jess. It's sure somethin' that he's our president after forty years in the Army and not a lick of political experience. I guess his views are so vague and his smile so big that rivals get disarmed. The name Eisenhower seems like mother, heaven, and home to most of us. He did it for us in Europe, you know, our supreme commander, and now we can do it for ourselves at home around this lake. We'll make it with a few smarts, a lot of sweat, and hope that the fish bite and the boaters keep wanting to play on the water. We can make some money off that, you know. I love the lake!"

"Sure, Bert," was her cautious response, "but don't quit that mill job in Youngstown you just got. Even though it's twenty miles one way in your old truck, they do pay on a regular basis. That helps a lot with our paying the bills!"

Bert had been a Merchant Marine in the big war. His dream now was to be a merchant to fishermen, a marina owner and operator, filling the tanks of their thirsty boats and loading the tackle boxes that sat under their seats. He also would sell various things to the folks who pulled water skiers and cruised the lake in powerful boats, like the painted horses up on land circling happily on their way to nowhere. People's lives had been on hold too long. The war was over and it was play time! But the play could come only in between hard bouts of survival work for most folks, including the Kraemers.

While some people had extra money and spare time, Bert and Jessica didn't have much of either. No matter. They were determined to build a new life along the western shore of Lake Milton. Bert didn't quit his mill job—those big places had been booming with steel production during the war and still were, now cranking out mostly goods for domestic use. He would drive and labor in those big, noisy, hot, dirty places, but they weren't his dream. That was out at the lake.

Bert never was a dreamer out loud. People tended to know him as a dedicated and hardworking plodder who kept his feelings inside. One evidence of him dreaming was his actually building a little marina. It was at the mouth of a small bay not three blocks from the park and only five from his house. The sign he proudly erected said, "Bert's Bait and Berth Marina." People could rent space to keep their boats, and, of course, fill them up with gas and gear when it was time to hit the waves. That was his life's passion--fishing and supplying others doing the same.

The dream was big, but the reality was limited to a little wooden building and six docks, one with a gas pump. Inside the building were the big sellers, minnows, worms, plugs, pop, and candy bars. That was in the summertime, with a teenager or two hired to run the place until Bert could get home from the mill each day. It seemed like a lifetime that Bert had to spend in those steel mills in Youngstown, sweating and just waiting to get home—hone to the marina instead of really staying at home in the evenings. He didn't spend much time with his family.

Jessica struggled with this and began asking herself hard questions. "Bert needs to work hard, sure, but why so little time at home with me and little Bud? It's like he loves us but doesn't want to live with us. Why stay to himself so much?"

While they didn't talk about it most of the time, Bert's line of thought was obviously different. "Why not mostly the marina? The heat, dirt, drudgery, and danger of the mill in Youngstown makes coming home to the lake in my pick-up truck each evening a little journey to my true joy. Those twenty miles change my worlds, taking me to my own little clearing, my secret place of comfort."

The truth was that he had another reason for keeping so much to himself. He knew this terrible other reason very well, but tried so hard not to think about it. Jessica was sure it must exist, but she couldn't ever get him to talk about it. As the years dragged by, she wondered and worried more and more about what it was. He seemed to drift away from her, and from Bud too. He was kind and honest enough, but a big, strong man who was paralyzed by something and wasn't quite ever there for his family. The nagging complaint of Jessica was that she was being left mostly alone, isolated and lonely in the little village.

She didn't have her own car, so usually she was stranded. She could walk most places in the village that were really necessary, like to Sinclair's store, but that tiny world was soon a cramping bore. She hadn't seen the bigger world like Bert—although she longed to. It didn't look good for her in the long-term since there was little choice but to buy into

Bert's lowered horizons and limited affections. Maybe she could build something into Bud and hope that one day it would send him far away and she could go along. Jessica couldn't even get a job of her own, both because there were virtually no local opportunities and because Bert was opposed to the woman of the house working outside—it would mark him as an inadequate bread winner for the family.

Lake Milton might have been culturally backward by most standards, but it wasn't the worst kind of place for a boy to grow up. It had lots of play possibilities not available in the much bigger Newton Falls some six miles away. That's where Bud was born during the war while Bert had been away fighting and Jessica was living in a little rented place and working to get by—her working was alright in Bert's eyes while the war was on and he couldn't be home, but not afterwards. Jessica and Bert, mostly Jessica, had decided on the name "Bud" when the birth was near. It suggested a flower bursting forth with new life and beauty, something so welcome amid the massive ugliness and widespread death of a world gone mad. The Kraemers would soon need plenty of budding.

Housing was scarce right after the war, very scarce, so this family had gone the six miles out to Lake Milton where a little summer cottage was available. It was cheap, for good reasons, but at least it existed. Just getting it winterized required Bert's best carpentry efforts. It could get quite cold and snowy in that area of northeast Ohio, with the blizzards sometimes spilling off Lake Erie and reaching that far south. It could also get hot in the summer, ideal for frolicking in the park and on the lake. The fishing was quite good. It had been a new and hopeful beginning.

Craig Beach village was a tiny place, only a fraction of the population in nearby Newton Falls—which wasn't all that much either. But even in the village the boys and girls had a decent place to go to school. Price-town was less than three miles from the Beach and a bus went right to its door after going around the northern end of the lake where the dam was. Bert, Jessica, and Bud Kraemer had settled in to build a life. It was almost ten years after their first arrival when the magic of the clearing in the woods had first happened for Bud.

The secluded magic was very different from the very public magic of the dance hall in the park. On summer evenings, guest bands or singers would sometimes strut their stuff in there. After Elvis Presley had made his first appearances on TV and cut his first records, the music of the new king of Rock 'n' Roll could be heard in much of the village late into the evening. Bud rarely went inside this hall, thought by his parents to be like the adjacent bowling alley, a hangout for the local riffraff. Presley never came to the village personally, of course, but his music quickly made it to this little out-of-the-way place.

A quiet kid like Bud, banned from the inside of the hall, could still wander through the park to the beat of "Jailhouse Rock" or "Hound Dog." Sometimes he would walk right past the little kiosk where the palm reader tried to lure folk—"A quarter for your future!" He wondered if that was all it was worth. He never went in and disappeared behind the heavy-looking curtain. He wanted to keep his quarter, when he had one, and he half believing the rumor that some who went in never came out!

The bowling alley in the Craig Beach amusement park was privately owned, as was the whole park, and it was not always in the best of repair. It had some troubled boards behind the neat rows of duck pins, ten per lane that had to be set up by hand after every successful ball had rolled down the long, shiny wood planks. A little platform above the pins is where a young employee would sit, waiting to step down and re-set the game after pins had been struck and flown wildly just below his feet. That outside wall just behind the platform was water damaged from the years of delayed maintenance, resulting in rotted wood near ground level. Pin setters appreciated the draft the opening allowed. It could get very hot back there!

Not two hundred or so feet beyond the rotted wall, just beyond the park grounds, lurked in silence a local mystery. Bud had seen the place from a distance lots of times, but had never gotten close. His view was from an opposite street, not down the lanes and through the old boards. That would have required his being inside where he wasn't allowed. Bowling cost money and some of the bigger kids who had money hung around the lanes and smoked. So Bud stayed away because he couldn't afford the cost and wasn't allowed that close to the "sin" of his school friends.

The Kraemers weren't church-going people, but they had a strong Christian family history of the conservative kind that put cigarettes in a body-destroying and God-offending category. They were dirty, smelly, and expensive, and definitely not for Bud, even though his father smoked all the time (and secretly wished he didn't). At least one boy of the next generation could be protected from a sin that brought sickness.

The mystery behind the bowling alley was a pond, dark on the surface, barely big enough for a boat to row about, squeezed into an isolated space that was shielded from the nearby houses by fields of weeds and briars that no one ever touched. Kids like Delores lived only a block away. They usually avoided this likely stagnant pool, both because their parents feared a drowning and they had heard the stories—maybe made up, but maybe not. A friend asked Delores how deep it was. Her answer didn't clear up much.

"The pool is about ten feet deep, or maybe a hundred," she said. "Nobody really knows or has the nerve to try and find out. Water quality is too poor to sustain life, or it's so loaded with food that the monster might be real, full, and dangerous." Stories didn't agree, and conservationists had never checked. Word was that the property belonged to someone in Youngstown who never came to Craig Beach and might have even forgotten the useless little backwater place.

Delores made quite an announcement to Bud on the school bus one day. "People have seen things at night in this pond, Bud, large green eyes on the water's surface that had been startled by a flashlight!" Bud didn't know whether to laugh or shake with fear.

"You're making that up!"

"Are you sure about that, Bud?" He wasn't, of course.

There also were conflicting opinions in the village, even among adults, some saying that those claiming sightings had more imagination than good sense and truthful mouths. Others dared not tempt fate by offending whatever might be there. When Halloween came, kids with their begging bags roamed the area, even after dark, but always in groups, and never too close to the pond. Parents weren't taking chances and gave strict orders. No one had ever seen the thing come out of the pond to chase anyone. Still, as Delores told Bud, "there's always a first time, and I think it's hungry!"

The story Delores told was more convincing than what some of the other kids were saying. People trusted her judgment. She came from a good family that lived so close to the pond that stray sounds in the night could easily escape from down there and quickly reach the girl's bedroom window—kept open in the summer, with only a screen to filter out the flies and any larger monsters in the world.

"Did something happen, Delores?" asked Bud.

"Well, yes. One winter day I slipped down to the pond's bank on my sled. The water was frozen solidly and I wanted a nice ride. With all that ice, there was no way out for the monster. It was like there was a frozen lid on his cage, except for the one spot where my foot broke through! I was instantly chilled in the icy water." Bud's face flushed.

"Keep going, Delores, what happened then?"

"Then's when the worst thing happened, not more ice breakage or my mom's feared drowning. Despite the cold, I still could feel it. It was something awful. 'Ouch!' I yelled."

The girl's outcry could be heard for some distance, which could have gotten her in big trouble. It was full daylight and she had been where she knew she shouldn't be. To satisfy Bud's curiosity, she kept the story rolling.

"It had been a sharp sting on my foot, some scary blood, and a fast trip home. I inspected my foot in private, saw the puncture wound, and wondered how it had gotten there. And how would I explain all this to my parents?"

"Had the edge of the ice cut your foot?"

"Nope. It was a puncture, like a big tooth bite. Maybe it was a nail in a piece of driftwood trapped under the ice. Probably. Or, of course, maybe not. It certainly could've been the bite of the monster that didn't appreciate the disturbance from above, and naturally it would've been really hungry that time of year. I didn't dare share this possibility with my parents; they just assumed the nail theory, treated my wound, and really scolded me for having been in such a dangerous place."

You'd think that a mystery pool like that, just blocks away from Bud's house, would have fascinated him. It did, but only to a point. Delores telling him about the likely tooth attack in that watery monster's lair should have been the center of the things flying in and out of Bud's fertile imagination for days. But not so. He liked Delores, and enjoyed the thrill of her (silly?) story, but something more dramatic for him soon came to occupy his mind. It was his dog that he loved, and especially that little secret place that Lucky had led him to one fateful day. There were no monsters there, but for him the place was heavy with mystery, heavy enough to distract from monster tales. And, of course, for him there was that secret resident who showed up sometimes.

The simplest of things had gotten it all started. "Good boy!" Bud loved his black and white Spaniel. Praising him was as natural as eating and sleeping.

"You've got him, Lucky!" The dog had cornered a little pest that now wouldn't pester anymore. Lucky had chased it into the woods and nailed it behind a bush. When Bud had parked his bike and caught up on foot, the dog's tail was wagging with excitement. The chase was over and, for the boy as well as the dog, a special place had been discovered. The find was more important than could be imagined at the time. Forget the murky pool and rumors of a foot-biting monster; this was a misty marvel of unlimited proportions. The fact that it looked like nothing at all made it easy for Bud to keep it all for himself.

He was in the fourth grade when he first found this place—or, with Lucky's help, it found him. It really seemed that way, a place anxious to be known and loved by Bud, a location coated with a seeking mind of its own. The discovery was safe. As a loyal dog, Lucky licked Bud's face and promised to show nobody where it was. This secret location was soon visited as often as possible. It was Bud's own port from which he could sail to other worlds. It was a much-loved little get-away, his boyish version of his dad's marina dream, a magic place for hiding from harsh realities, and sometimes sailing into the mists of mystery.

Delores may have gotten her foot wet, cold, and punctured by something when it slipped down into the pond's dreaded darkness, but Bud would be getting much more. He would be getting his heart full and warm as he flew upward into the light of distant skies, launched unexplainably from his private place of amazing insight. She had been stabbed under that water by the fangs of something, and he would gain an unpleasant scar or two himself while on his celestial journeys. The pains of growing up and the search for wisdom sure have their risks!

One thing certainly scared Bud. Something bad would happen at school about once a month. Afterwards, he would long for the solace of his get-away place. Things frightened him more than the other kids, maybe because of his sensitive nature, but mostly because of his unsettled home life. Even so, nobody liked this periodic happening. Some of the kids would watch the "Today Show" on TV before school. Its host, Dave Garroway, would end by holding up his big right hand and offering the sincere benediction, "Peace." Everyone hoped for peace in the world, but knew that it was under threat again. This time it was Russia with its atomic bomb.

The teacher would get it started. She knew that it was bomb-drill time, so she would shout without warning, "DUCK AND COVER!" Maybe it was a pathetic exercise in futility, but it's all the school knew to do. The Russians could be dropping the dreaded bomb on nearby Youngstown or Warren, or even on their precious dam only a few hundred yards away! Kids were to protect themselves by getting under their seats the best they could and covering their heads with their bare hands, staying there until they got the all-clear signal. It was a self-defense drill, mandatory by school policy.

It really scared Bud each time it happened—he knew that it certainly wouldn't have protected him from an actual bomb! He finally decided that things at school aren't always connected to the real world very well. As soon as he would get home after a drill day, if the weather and his mother allowed, he would head for his very private place to hide and imagine and dream. He convinced himself that he was really safe here. The big trees were like huge hands covering his head better than he could do at school during the drill. And better yet, the Russians couldn't find him out here—the school could be seen from anywhere.

The park, loud music, French fries, the beach, the palm reader, and the marina of his dad's were down Beach Lane if you headed east from the Kraemer's house. They were semi-real places of amusement for industry-weary people from Youngstown and Akron and elsewhere. Bud's special place was the other way, westward toward the setting sun— although he was never allowed to go there when darkness was falling. It also might have been only semi-real, he was never sure, but it was real enough to serve well the occasional needs of a burdened little boy.

Reality is a shifting thing, so dependent on the perceiver. Who's to decide what's real? Aren't our personal realities merely the products of our own views of things? That's part of what Bud loved about this wooded place. It was what he knew it to be, what he needed it to be. Sometimes he would ride his bike to the edge of the woods and walk in to his secret clearing where he could count on being tingled and warmed by a fresh dose of comforting seclusion and mystery. The place was hidden by bushes crowded between several trees. To the non-believer, that's all there was. Bud was a believer, however, and he could get there from his house in two minutes, which for him was a quick journey that could reveal timeless things far, far away, even long, long ago.

His initial fascination with the place may have been encouraged by something that happened at school other than a scary drill. His teacher, Miss Mason, had started talking one day about a famous book by somebody named Thoreau. This strange man once had moved to the woods, somewhere out east. She explained that he wanted to live thoughtfully— whatever that meant. Apparently, he had wondered what nature, quiet, and simplicity have to offer in the way of peace and wisdom. This Thoreau fellow feared facing death and realizing that he'd never actually lived. So the odd guy had decided that we sleepy humans have to reawaken ourselves, shake off the shadowy life, and start expecting a dawn— which is to be found best when alone in the woods living as simply as possible. In Thoreau's case, the dawns arrived by some pond called "Walden." Bud wondered if Delores called her pond "Thunder Hole" or "Fang Central"—hardly a place to experience gentle dawns!

That little classroom story had been more than enough to stimulate Bud's imagination. It might have sent him to Delores to talk more about her pond, but it didn't. That little spot with stagnant water and— maybe—a snorting monster was reserved for her. He had his own place where it was strangely and safely quiet. Snuggled in this secure seclusion where Lucky had caught the pest, Bud determined to find the best for himself—whatever that was. For him, it was the Walden Pond of Craig

Beach village, the port from which ships left for everywhere and always seemed to have a ticket for him. It was there that young Bud Kraemer could start pondering his real inner thoughts, and they weren't all about girls and homework. Some were painful and persistent.

Even though he loved his parents, Bud doubted that they or his friends would ever understand or even believe the places he had begun going once safely in the clearing. And he really did go, not only to the clearing, but far beyond. These ventures were all very real to Bud. They offered ways of survival when life got to be just too much. And, unfortunately, that "too much" was to be the lot of Bud's family most of the time.

Chapter Four

LAZY SUSANS

Bud already could see the nursing home glaring at him again. It was a place of pain that seemed to be insisting on his return. There was no hiding from this harsh reality. Now a grown man, he knew that no covering of his eyes or getting under some desk would change anything. Death was in the air and not to be denied.

Coming back this second time was no less sad and tense than the first time, but still necessary. The tension was because Bert Kraemer, that silent patient back in room 109, still might not be awake to share with him, might not even recognize him if awake, or might recognize him but refuse to accept his apologies. The man might or might not even still be alive! Words from the nurse at the reception desk brought a little reassurance.

"You're his son, right?" Bud nodded affirmatively, feeling a rare touch of pure pride that indeed he was Bert's son.

"Yes, he's alive—and maybe awake. Check with the nurse back there. Go right on in." The receptionist's words were welcome, but her tone told him that there was no guarantee about anything, at least not for long. Bud was angry at fate or whoever schedules life's departures. They come too soon and are so final.

"He just can't die until we've talked," thought Bud. "Even if he's on his way to a better place, and I certainly can't be sure of that, some repair of this present place needs done first!"

Maybe all of us empty and hurting humans need a place away, a hideout reserved just for us, a destiny of well-deserved rest, a wardrobe door that opens magically into a world of good and bad witches and a lordly lion who saves the day. Such a Narnia fantasy place might make the difference as we hunt for hope and vision, things not easily available in the ordinary crush of public places. Especially when we face danger, transition, especially death, shouldn't there be a special somewhere reserved just for us, maybe to the west toward the setting sun, a place not far into a nearby woods where memories of older days still linger and the seeds of future days can get planted?

"For Dad," Bud pondered lovingly, "maybe there will be a mystical marina beside a crystal lake, a heavenly place where the fish always bite and the mosquitoes never do. I wish that for him. May his life dreams finally come true."

Whatever. Bud now sat down at his dad's bedside and waited as patiently as he could. Bert was quiet, peaceful looking, but alive. For now, at least, there still would be no communication with him. A nurse said she had given Mr. Kraemer something which made him both comfortable and a little out-of-it. That shot was Bert's momentary door to a more relaxed and probably deserved elsewhere. Nothing to do now but go out to the lounge, try to get comfortable, and wait. Just sitting there, of course, didn't keep Bud's mind and memories from troubling him. He began to reflect back.

In Bud's younger years, it hadn't been east Belfast, Ireland, that fired his imaginary world, like it did for the Narnia and Aslan tales of C. S. Lewis. Only recently had Bud even heard of Lewis or read about the wardrobe and witches. What now filled his memory wasn't the mysterious pond behind the park's bowling alley and near the side yard where Delores lived. The place igniting his imagination was a very simple spot, not eastward toward the pond, but westward on Beach Lane and then into the woods about fifty yards. If his dad could've gotten his truck on that spot, there would've been little space left to even sit down.

"Morning Glen" is what StarWalker had called it. It was very close to home and, at the same time, very far away, almost like leaving home as the best way of finally coming home. If Lewis could shut kids in an imaginary wardrobe and then imagine almost anything emerging beyond its backside, releasing the kids into a frozen fantasy land, why not little Bud on the edge of Craig Beach? Couldn't he go to amazing places? That Thoreau fellow had his pond and woods, and for Bud there had been the village clearing and, of course, StarWalker.

Bud's trance was broken briefly by an unexpected voice. "Want something to drink, Mr. Kraemer?" An attendant had seen him staring out the window and knew he might have to be there awhile longer. He squirmed in the chair a little, getting oriented back to the present.

"No thanks. Just busy thinking until Dad wakes up, thinking about when I was a kid around here." Bud looked back out the lounge window and his childhood memories started flowing again.

He was once told at school that he was growing up in the "Western Reserve" originally set aside for the state of Connecticut. It was to be a place out west where that eastern coastal state could put extra or unwanted citizens. That escape-valve territory was now his home, his personal reserve. But that little bit of American history trivia had spawned troubling questions.

"Had I and my family been rejects in the East, people not wanted anymore? Was I a misfit, a castoff, someone not appreciated by the good people of polite society? Was I too weak to take care of myself on the school bus and at school when bullies like Mike Jakas started their prowling around and smelled an easy target when the Kraemer kid came in sight?" These were troubling thoughts for a boy with a shaky self-image to start with.

Whatever the answers, for Bud there was a memory that was coming back to him. It was a tiny and yet wonder-full Ohio reserve in the great big reserve of this Connecticut state. Lying just west of his house on Beach Lane, and mercifully set aside by someone just for him and his thoughts, the secret place, the fairyland western reserve, the Morning Glen was definitely there. It had been enjoyed by a boy and his dog Lucky and, of course, by his special, ancient friend that no one else knew existed.

"Was the old Indian the emptiness of a mirage or the fullness of a miracle? Maybe time would tell. Maybe not. Maybe the question wasn't even important. Maybe it was the most important question of all. Who knew?" One thing was all too clear to Bud. His father had an unnamed problem. It was big and life-long and unknown to others.

Bert hadn't shared much of himself over the years, even with his own family, and now he wasn't talking at all, a dying man fighting for mere consciousness. But back then, when Bud was young, on a rare occasion Bert did talk a little about the recent war, although nothing about his personal involvement. Once he told Bud that, years after the war had ended, there were still Japanese soldiers hidden in caves and underground tunnels in the Philippines. They hadn't gotten the news that the war was over, or they didn't believe it. They were still ready to fight, afraid to come out, living in a world that no longer existed. How strange! How pathetic!

Bud remembered wondering about that sad circumstance and how it might relate to his own dad. After all, Bud and his mom had always wished that Bert would act differently toward them, live openly in the moment and not be so closed and distant about his time in the war and his most inner thoughts. For some painful reason, that just wasn't his way. Bud had felt mostly fatherless; Jessica barely had a husband, at least one meeting her personal needs.

Bud stared out the window of the nursing home and wondered. "Was that business about Japanese still in caves a picture of his own dad in a sad way—something from that war still active in Bert's mind that had crippled his life to this very day? Was the war still not over for him either? For that matter, was StarWalker also nothing but a pathetic leftover from some difficult yesterday? Had he been the only survivor of some Indian war that he thought was still going on? Or was this Indian living in the most real of all worlds, a spirit world—or was the old man living at all?"

Reality can be a slippery and confusing business, especially for a sensitive and hurting little boy. And, unfortunately, Bud had kept his inner thoughts from his dad over the years. Isn't that what his dad always had done, stay inside himself? One wrong tends to spawn another. Bert was a strong and honest man, hardworking, but so poor at sharing his real self with others. Was the war really over for him? Whatever the answer, the secret clearing had been a good place for Bud.

"If Dad won't talk, and Mom keeps struggling without answers either, I'll just go there." He would be there on some summer evenings, playing with his treasured pocketknife or trying to fill a jar with the magical light of fireflies. He would sometimes stare at them and wonder if they knew something he didn't.

When at home, sometimes Bud would watch Fess Parker playing Davy Crockett on the family TV that sprouted rabbit ears—later the Kraemers got a big outdoor antenna. When they did, Bud got a new job. He would be sent outside to twist the tall pole back and forth to shift the direction of the big prongs on its top and hopefully improve the reception inside. Someone in the house would yell, "That's better! Keep it right there and come on in." The voice usually was his mom's; his dad often had other things to do.

Bud once wondered if his dad had ever seen a submarine during the war. It wasn't hard for a boy to imagine that antenna he was always twisting being a periscope sticking up in the ocean of air, peeking over the top, trying to find a target. Finally, that pole and its fickle prongs could be teased into delivering the desired signal from Akron, Youngstown, or Cleveland. It just had to be spun at the right angle, with proper allowance for the strength and direction of the wind. The Crockett show finally would become clearer, exciting a boy for his own woods adventures.

And for Bud, it would be Crockett on the screen and not the other stuff usually watched by the people across the street. Over there, the Halsteads had a really good TV and different program tastes. They even had an electronic box inside the house that automatically turned the ariel outside. Wow!

The odd thing was that Hazel and Frank watched religious programs when they could. Fulton J. Sheen was a Catholic favorite on the new tube, and that's what the Halsteads were, Catholics. Sheen was formal in his fancy robe, a bishop of some kind. He sounded so wise, and still was really funny, a fascinating combination. But there also was a new Baptist evangelist on TV. He was interesting in quite a different way—a Billy Graham fellow that Catholics were discouraged from watching.

Bud knew all this because Hazel was quite a talker and told him about it in the yard one day. He went right home and told his mom.

"Hey, Mom, Mrs. Halstead said that Billy Graham is a very enthusiastic preacher. Even though he's every inch a Protestant, and apparently not loyal to the pope who lives a long way off in Rome, she doesn't care. She watches what she wants and dares the priest to catch her! Do you think we're going to have trouble in the village, like a religious war or something?"

"I doubt it, Bud. We have enough else to worry about. Hazel's OK, quite a character, but aren't we all in our own ways? And don't worry about the priest. He never bothers Protestants."

The subject of formal religion in general was mostly a bore to the Kraemers. They were Protestants by tradition, and of a conservative brand, but these days they were hardly enthusiastic about it all. Sheen or Graham? Crockett was good enough to watch. Bud thought Milton Berle was funnier than any of them, and a good laugh was important regardless of how it came.

Their religious indifference included more than avoiding the Catholic parish down the road—where the Halsteads belonged. They also ignored the little Protestant church on the opposite side of the lake from Craig Beach. Jessica thought it was Baptist, maybe connected to Graham somehow. Bud had seen that tiny building a few times—he didn't often get over to that side of the lake. Ed Sinclair, the pastor, was surely one of the more colorful characters in the village, a favorite of the kids. Part of Ed's fascination was that he was missing his left arm. He told a story about an accident during the war, something called "friendly fire." He did have a stump almost down to where the elbow had been, and he could use it rather well. It was funny to watch sometimes.

Ed was the grocer in the village as well as a pastor, "bi-vocational" he called himself. At first Bud thought it meant that he could write with either hand—even though he had only one! Ed enjoyed saying that he provided people with food for the belly and eternal food for the soul. He'd been known to give a free ice cream cone to a kid on a hot day, and he was sometimes seen at Bert's marina just chatting about whatever. Bud sometimes wondered why his dad would talk to this man more than to his own family.

Ed's wife, Joyce Sinclair, was rather quiet and worked in the store, giving Ed the time for the soul part of his work. She knew Bud's mom, but they didn't talk much for whatever reason. That lack of social activity by Jessica Kraemer extended to other women in the village too, something Bud often wondered about—even worried about. Bud could figure out a way to worry about almost everything.

"Why doesn't my mom just hang around places and visit like other village women do? There isn't much of anything else to do in the village, that's for sure. But she stays at home even when there's nothing to do there. She seems so sad most of the time. I wish I knew why and could fix it."

Bud often reflected on his mom's reclusive manner. He tried hard not to get depressed himself. When not on an errand to Sinclair's store for his mom, he likely was in the clearing if weather allowed, sometimes pretending to be Davy Crockett, roaming the woods, befriending the natives, working for justice—he even had a Davy lunch box for carrying to school. The clearing was a spawning place for different worlds and times, a place where Bud's mysterious friend sometimes showed up and told him things about amazing yesterdays. When his old friend talked, Bud could see faces and hear voices that still wanted to communicate about experiences of some distant yesterday that apparently had some meaning for today.

Some of those faces were smiling when he saw them; many others were crying, sometimes even screaming! They were like a cloud of witnesses hanging over today, a crowd of people from elsewhere who weren't done with this life yet. They weren't threatening, although sometimes they were scary to an emotionally fragile boy. They would tend to watch Bud, wanting to help him, shedding their tears of experience and their droplets of wisdom, sometimes in a gentle rain and sometimes in violent bursts of thunder and lightning. StarWalker, the old Indian, usually spoke for them. Bud didn't make all this up, he really didn't.

A startling buzzer went off. Bud snapped back to present reality and realized that it was the signal for residents in the nursing home, at least the ones who could walk or roll their wheelchairs, to make their way to the cafeteria for lunch. A kind nurse came over to him and asked if he'd like to join them. He declined politely. Watching these poor people didn't encourage an appetite.

The nurse had been kind enough to check for Bud. "I'm sorry, Mr. Kraemer, that you've had to keep waiting. Your father should be awake soon. We'll let you know. Come on down to the cafeteria if you change your mind."

It was only seconds before Bud's mind left the activity around him and reverted back to his boyhood. He recalled once imagining a huge expansion of a simple device in the little kitchen at home. His mother called it a "lazy Susan"—a lot better name than "dumbwaiter" that he heard his dad call it. Bert had built it for Jessica's convenience, so he really didn't mean dumb. It was quite clever and his dad was secretly proud of it, but never actually said so. Bud wondered, "Why does Dad cover up his real feelings? I know he does sometimes, I can tell."

Oh well, back to that lazy Susan. It wasn't lazy at all—in fact, it helped the lady in the kitchen be more lazy. It was three curved shelves stacked about a foot apart. They could all move together in a circle, spinning around a vertical pole with the push of a hand. Lots of kitchen supplies could be stored on those shelves, with the ones needed at the time being easily brought to the front. A little spin and all was well!

"It was more than clever; it could be plain fun," Bud thought to himself. Once, when he was alone, he made it spin and spin and spin. All he wanted was to see it go. That excitement started the boy thinking more about this thing in the kitchen.

"This cute device of mom's reminds me of something. I know. It's the merry-go-round down Beach Lane from my house. Half of the kids in the village can get on it at the same time, stored happily out of their parent's hair. All you have to do is wait for a few seconds and everybody will spin right to you. I've watched a kid wait for the horse he wanted to ride glide right into reach. He jumped on it and galloped away to the sound of the music. What a life! Of course, you're supposed to wait until the ride is over to get on or off. It's safer that way, but a bit of danger only adds to the fun!"

One day Bud's teacher had been trying to explain the meaning of a metaphor, so Bud decided that these were metaphors—the lazy Susan in the kitchen, the merry-go-round in the park, even the clearing of his. That spot in the woods was kind of Bud's personal lazy Susan to the past—and even the future. It worked in an amazing way if you were there and could understand. Scenes of earlier generations would spin into Bud's view and reach, with the one most full of wisdom for the moment stopping right in front of him. When it stopped, StarWalker sometimes would be there to do the talking for yesterday.

The first time Bud met StarWalker was startling to say the least. It was a warm afternoon, nearly suppertime. Shadows had begun to lengthen a little in part of the clearing. Bud was upset because his mom and dad had argued, and right in front of him. She had hoped for some time together and he felt compelled to spend the evening at the marina instead.

Suddenly, he was just standing there! He was every inch an Indian, although nothing about his posture was threatening. Did the TV give the wrong impression of real Indians? The rugged red skin of his face quickly softened into a smile.

"Hello, Bud Kraemer, my name is StarWalker. I sensed that you needed me, so I've come. Please don't be afraid. I'll sit down right here by this tree trunk and you stay where you are over there. We'll talk a little after you manage to close your mouth and quit breathing so hard."

They sat there for a minute or two, just looking at each other. Bud felt so exposed with only his shorts and sneakers on and no help that he could call on immediately—except for Lucky who, amazingly, didn't even bark at this old man. He surely would have if he sensed danger to his master. Bud finally did manage to say something.

"What did you say your name is?"

"StarWalker, my son. Good dog you have there, and sorry about the trouble at home today. You'll understand all about that someday, but only when you're much older."

"How do you know about my family?"

"That's hard to explain. I hope that my knowing helps you from time to time. Assuming that we do meet once in a while, and always here, let's give this little place a name. We'll call it *Morning Glen*, little Bud, because it's the quiet, green, growing place where new things are born and new light shines for you, where memories of yesterday will come alive and the sun rises on new meaning and hope—and just for you!"

"OK, Mr. Indian, sorry, StarWalker, that sounds nice, crazy nice, but I'm scared. I'm not so sure if you're safe to be around."

"I understand, Bud. People fear evil spirits, and ghosts, and vampires in isolated spots, almost anything unknown; but you, little Bud, you should learn that here, with me, in Morning Glen, you can be safe and even meet the Great Spirit who is wisdom and love. That Great Spirit says that sometimes we are to be still, for only in the stillness will we ever come to know some important things. There's nothing to fear, my son, and lots to learn." Bud finally was relaxing, still not quite sure who this old but kind man really was.

There was something hurtful inside Bud in those younger years—maybe there still was as he continued to wait and fear his dad's death. It was a spiritual vacuum not satisfied when he was a boy. The village routines were merely eating, cutting the lawn, feeding the dog, riding his bike, watching a little TV, finishing daily homework from school, and going out back of the house to pick up those hard little apples on the ground and throw them into the distant trees, pretending to be a famous pitcher for the Cleveland Indians. That 1954 baseball team had been amazing with its four, yes, four twenty-game winners, Mike Garcia, Bob Feller, Bob Lemon, and Early Wynn.

What a great bunch those men were! Bud wished he could go far away and be somebody important like that. But he had always been bothered by more serious things, like boys maybe shouldn't be, or maybe should be. They ranged well beyond baseball.

What was this talk about God and the pope and Billy Graham? Why do people have to die? Why did so many die in the big war, but not his dad? Why did Mr. Sinclair have that awful thing happen to his arm? Why did his mom cry so hard sometimes and try to hide it from her son? It was such a little house and he could hear very well. Everybody seemed to respect and even love Jessica, but only at a distance. Somehow things just weren't right for her and she hurt inside. She avoided lots of people, especially Maggie Welch across the lake, and for no reason Bud could see. Maggie was a very nice lady. And, of course, why did he wonder about so many things when his friends didn't seem to?

Bud did care, care deeply, and just couldn't forget what his teacher had said once about Langston Hughes, a man who had written a curious little poem. It was about a "colored" boy at a carnival—almost like the park down Beach Lane. Everybody Bud knew had white skin, but this poem was about a boy from the South where apparently whites and coloreds weren't allowed to sit side-by-side on the school bus. A few lines went...

> On the bus we're put in the back—
> But there ain't no back
> To a merry-go-round!
> Where's the horse
> For a kid that's black?

"Now that's really odd," thought Bud. "It's true! A merry-go-round treats everybody the same—no front, no back. Everybody is going the same place—nowhere, and all at the same speed. Do the colored horses care about the color of their riders? Why do adults tend to be mean to each other, creating backs of buses and then assigning them to lesser people? Who gets to decide who's lesser, and why would they do that anyway?"

Maybe Bud could get an answer in the secret place. He knew that he should be still and wait patiently if he expected StarWalker to show. And, so StarWalker had once said, maybe he should also wait for some "Great Spirit."

"By the way," Bud thought, "isn't StarWalker some other color than the standard and respectable white? On TV, the cowboys were always the up-front good guys, the white guys, sometimes even on white horses, like the Lone Ranger who was the best of the best guys. The other guys were 'redskins.' Should they go to the back of the bus with the black boys? Why would God create people of two classes in the first place, good and less than good, front-seat and back-seat people? Why isn't the world a merry-go-round where there are no back seats? Why doesn't the Lone Ranger wear a white mask, the superior color?"

There weren't any kids at the Pricetown school with black skin, certainly not teachers. Bud's dad said there were plenty of them in the mills in Youngstown. They had drifted North to get jobs, dirty, non-skilled, often dangerous jobs mostly—and they were rough people and not to be trusted. Bud wondered the obvious.

"Should these different people be allowed to have horses or not? If they had them, and really good, white ones, would they be made dangerously strong and hurt the good white people? Is color of skin really a sign of the good and bad?"

And then there were the people Bert called "Japs," short for people from Japan—a category of hated lesser types. They actually were short, Bud had been told, both in stature and worthiness as full human beings. This, he decided, was left-over propaganda from the war, stuff Bert carried around and kept inside. There was that and more, an unnamed more that troubled his dad. But Bud never dared ask about it. He was sure his dad wouldn't tell him if he did.

"If there 'ain't no back' on the merry-go-rounds of this world," wondered Bud, "should we make some back so we have somewhere proper to put the lesser people? Isn't that what Craig Beach is, a dumping place for Connecticut? Did that mean that the villagers were the same as Blacks and Japs to good Connecticut people?"

A big bird flew by, right in Bud's line of sight out the nursing home window. It broke his concentration. So, he rubbed his eyes and decided that he'd had enough of this remembering for now. Surely his dad would wake up soon and be able to talk, but apparently not yet. How long? He decided to stay open to more remembering, always hoping for one more chance with his dad. A serious conversation was so important! After staring out the window a minute or two more, the first of several more wandering thoughts took hold of him.

"Color and place must not be all of it. I'm white on the outside and still I feel like one of the lessers inside myself. And some of the kids back then treated me like I was black or red or some other unacceptable color. And Mom was certainly white, and she cried a lot, almost like she was always being forced to be in the back of something. What was wrong with her that never went away to her dying day? And what's wrong with me, and Dad?" Sure, he's dying now, but why has he been kind of dead inside for years and years?" Maybe Bud would find out soon, finally, or maybe not.

Chapter Five

THE DOOMED

It was like a warm womb, a wish-filled wonderland, and occasionally a theater of terror. Bud Kraemer would certainly never forget this time in Morning Glen. It was a summer day in his make-believe Narnia, a place that in some ways might be more real than the supposed reality of the routine, hollow, kept-inside, and cried-over lives that many people in the village seemed to be living—especially his own parents.

It was his secret Walden-like place in the woods, his own country, his own train station where he had a private pass to everywhere. He had been with his parents once to meet a train arriving at the station in Warren. He was thrilled by the size and power of that big machine and the far-away places the schedule said it went. He stood within fifty feet of it as it rolled into the station, and he remembered feeling his ears roar and the earth tremble under his feet.

"Wow!" It just flew out of his mouth. He wished he could go somewhere, anywhere.

Being in the clearing made him feel special, a master train conductor, singular, safe, truly himself in a way that he couldn't explain to anyone else or experience anywhere else. He didn't even try; it was his business and nobody else's. He wasn't entirely comfortable with talk of a "Great Spirit," but he wasn't opposed to it either since it made him curious and feel connected to something bigger. At least he could be sure that Star-Walker was kind and wise. And Bud had lots of questions.

Can the world unseen by our eyes be as real and important as the stuff we look at with our little, fragile eyeballs? Does the heart have special eyes of its own? Are they buried somewhere deep in our chests? Is there reality at the level of feeling as well as reasoning? Should a rapidly growing boy like Bud be wasting time with such unanswerable questions?

Jessica Kraemer looked every day on the commonplace of small village life; it seemed to her like a prison sentence. There were no walls around the place, but to her it was her life's dead-end. Unlike Bud and his clearing, Jessica seemed to have nowhere to go for relief.

On one fateful day, Bud just couldn't get two things off his mind. The week before hadn't been good for him, not at all. He'd been sick at home and then shocked at school, a nasty combination. First was the sickness. It was truly frightening. Chicken pox was rather common, sure, but that didn't matter. When ugly sacks of gooey yellow stuff start hanging from your skin, people are afraid to get near you, and you're not allowed to go to school, it gets scary, even humiliating for a boy. Whatever chickens had been so kind as to share their pox with him, they'd done a great job and certainly weren't welcome!

Bud had missed a whole week of school. His mother was very attentive, freely risking her own health to care for his every need. It was a small crisis that gave her life temporary meaning. To Jessica, Bud was the hope she had given up for herself. Maybe one day he could get free of the village and really live in the bigger world. It might be too late for her, but if he got away, in her heart she would fly with him into the great beyond of somewhere else, anywhere else. His fulfillment she would gladly grasp as her own.

She'd cried hard one evening during Bud's sickness, feeling sorry for herself and fearing that her boy would get trapped in the village like her. Bert didn't hear her sobs—he was out back in his "shed" working on something, too distant and busy to notice. He wasn't mean, not at all, just preoccupied with himself and his many jobs. His family was nearly frantic with frustration. He'd been to sea, witnessed more of the world than he had wanted, and now appeared quite content with where they were and what he was doing—especially in his shed and at the marina.

Unfortunately, but as usual, Bud heard the crying—how couldn't he in that little house? He didn't understand, except that he knew his mother was very unhappy, and it hurt him terribly. She felt helpless, and he was beginning to feel helpless too, unable to do anything for her, even talk to her about it. He feared that he was inheriting whatever was plaguing her. His heart cried out for any answer. There was no response. He tried his own analysis based on boyish observations.

"If only Dad were more attentive to her, was willing to reassure her more, just talked to her about his deep feelings. Maybe if he'd hold her close as she cried, and even cried with her. That might help. Maybe." But that wasn't likely. It just wasn't Bert.

Bud did do one thing. He tried to lighten his mom's life, at least for a minute, by asking her a silly question. She'd stopped crying and was in the kitchen turning her lazy Susan to find something.

"Mom, can I have a quarter for the man crying down at the park?"

She was concerned, just as he intended: "Why's the poor man crying, Bud?"

"Well, Mom, he keeps crying out, 'Hot dog for a quarter! Hot dog for a quarter!" She laughed, not deeply, but at least momentarily. She so loved Bud and knew that he loved her, and it really hurt her to know that he knew and was trying to help somehow. She was in pain and trying to smile. She had a beautiful face, but one quickly getting wrinkles.

A boy shouldn't have to grow up trying to fix his parents! But Jessica couldn't explain her problems to her boy—she barely understood them herself. So she covered up her feelings as best she could and gave him a quarter for whatever he wanted to use it for. He was surprised and smiled gratefully—a quarter was real money!

"I was only teasing, Mom!"

"I know, my dear, but I want you to have it anyway." He decided to keep it as a symbol that he really was loved. He regularly assured her of that, and the quarter might help from time to time.

When he finally was allowed back on the bus and close to his friends, Bud was hardly made comfortable. First, it was the usual bully, Mike Jakas, a kid from the village who must have heard rumors and, as usual, decided to feel big by exploiting them. Swallowing strong feelings can make one choke deep inside. That's how Bud had to live sometimes, and Mike seemed to enjoy making it worse.

"Hey, Bud, you mama's boy. I hear your mom's a little weird! I also hear that getting near you can get other people really sick! Shouldn't you be in the back of the bus by yourself?" Mike knew he could get away with saying such an awful thing. He was tough and Bud was hardly the fighting type. Bud did the usual, all he knew. He looked away, embarrassed, trying to suffer in private, which Mike wouldn't let happen. Bud thought it through and made his move.

"I might as well be a 'colored' and go ahead and just sit back there. Maybe I'm really one of the lesser people in the world—and if not, going back there is safer anyway." He got up and moved back to a seat by himself. Betsy, seeing and hearing it all, was crying. She was a sensitive girl. She liked Bud and thought Mike was somewhere below the level of a jerk. She twisted around in her seat and caught Bud's eye for a second, trying to offer a little support. He noticed and wished she'd come back and sit with him—but then she'd likely get abused just like him. He sure didn't want that.

Arrival at the school couldn't come too soon on this day. But getting there didn't help Bud all that much. It started OK with Betsy brushing against him gently as she passed in him in the hall and said nothing. He knew she did it deliberately, trying to offer a friendly "Hi!" Without stirring up any more trouble, she wanted to reassure him that the whole world wasn't stupid.

Then came the new trouble. First it had been the chicken pox and isolation at home. Now it was a school shock. Mike's miserable mouth was soon compounded in its emotional impact on Bud by what the social studies teacher started telling his class that day. Bud was sitting in the front row—that was safer in the classroom, not like on the bus where he had to retreat to the back. The teacher was explaining that there once was a time in that area of northeast Ohio when there was a big Indian war. It was more like an outright massacre. It had completely changed the course of local history in that part of the Midwest.

Bud may not have gotten all the facts quite right, but he'd heard enough that his imagination was on the loose. He got off the bus after school and walked the short distance home. He greeted his mother—she was listening to the radio just killing time, waiting for Bert who'd eventually be home from the mill briefly before likely heading on to the marina. Then he rode his bike straight to Budland. He sometimes forgot that he was supposed to call it Morning Glen, but StarWalker would understand how intensely he now identified with the place.

While Bud hurried off to do his boyish thing, Jessica struggled with his going. She didn't understand why he so loved this secret place of his. She was jealous that his attention was being drawn away from her. In her loneliness, she always worried about where her boy actually was and whether someone else was stealing his affection. Bud had never tried to hide from her where he went, and she hoped he didn't ever lie. Her fear was that even her boy was abandoning her in his own way, finding something more compelling to do elsewhere.

Now Bud was there, sitting in silence, worrying about the lingering gore of dead Indians invading his sacred space, and looking up toward the tops of the big trees. They formed a protective canopy that softened the bright rays of the late-afternoon sun and sometimes seemed to be trying to gently filter life's harshness from him—a little like Betsy tried to do for Bud in the hall at school. The long wooden tree shafts were reaching toward and beyond that canopy, trying to grasp the wisdom or maybe even the wickedness embedded in the distant sky. Bits of scattered thoughts kept trying to peek between the highest branches, breaching the sense of protection, jabbing at Bud, and drifting down toward the floor of the earth with little shadows of doubt and fear. He huddled in a ball for warmth and an illusive feeling of safety.

Bud was afraid. Maybe everything is looking for a boy it can hurt. Maybe what he was seeing was only a mindless nothing. On the other hand, maybe it was only the stillness that comes just before a violent storm. Maybe another massacre was about to unleash its fury all over him. Was he safe out here all alone? In fact, was he really alone? Where was StarWalker when he really needed him?

Bud had just become a teenager and was a fertile field for things offering to stretch the mind. Sometimes the tall towers seemed to begin moving in unison, with the whole clearing turning faster and faster, like a dizzy clock hunting for the right time. A boy's consciousness can suddenly find itself on some celestial lazy Susan, moving, looking for the right place to stop, ready to serve up the goods of a yesterday that want to be seen and heard again.

Does yesterday have a mouth? Is history just another nasty Mike Jakas that won't go away? Tree trunks, even when not moving mysteriously, often seem to shimmer with sounds that only special woodland guests are allowed to hear. These particular trees probably made no noise at all except when Bud was there—he couldn't know for sure. His openness to things beyond the ordinary may have brought the sounds of silence into being. At least on this day, a scene was beginning to unfold before his eyes that threatened to burn some of the bark right off those trees. His dad was still in Youngstown working. His mom was home alone, as usual, probably listening to the radio and rummaging through magazines that allowed her to dream. Bud was in a better place--maybe.

Bud's thoughts headed toward the gruesome. "Might this very spot, this lovely stretch of green grass, have been the scene of many violent deaths? If I pushed aside some leaves, would I discover a huge pool of dried blood? Did they scalp each other? Are hunks of old hair still stuck somewhere in these very bushes around me? My chicken pox was bad enough, and Mike is sheer misery, but blood all over the place would be much worse!"

The clearing near Bud's home, surrounded by big trees, usually functioned as a protective shield over the disturbing moments of life, a welcome mask that could transform nasty events into almost anything Bud preferred. But not today. No one would prefer this Indian stuff flying around in his head. First it had been pox sloppily hanging on his body, and now it was scalps separated from heads and lying on the ground around him formed. Together they formed a truly sick mental brew. He hated its taste, shivered at its very appearance, but was being forced to drink and look anyway. The glory of the glen had turned gory.

Bud was being mysteriously transported into an old and terrible world, despite being barely two-hundred feet from the edge of Beach Lane. He was afraid to even look at a bush, a plain old bush. If he did, he might think he saw the shape of an Indian face in great pain. The face he wanted now was that of StarWalker, but he wasn't there.

"Oh, no!" Bud's eyes bulged. "There's no doubt about it now. This was worse than Mike's filthy mouth. This was all-out war!" It was Indians against Indians, ugliness everywhere, and not a cowboy in sight riding a white horse and ready to win the day. Nor was his teacher there to get the facts all straight for Bud. People were screaming, running, launching arrows, slashing throats with big knives, and horribly dying. Bud already knew that the Erie Indians would not survive this Iroquois onslaught. A prayer just flew out of his mouth.

Out of Bud's quivering mouth came a quick prayer. "Dear God, if you're up there, stop this thing if you can! And if it's finished history and can't be stopped or changed, at least seal my eyes and ears!"

But it wasn't stopping! Then, suddenly, there he was! Not God, and not one of the fighters, but somebody who was standing in the middle of the action, and yet somehow was remaining outside the fray. StarWalker finally had come! He was an old Indian, a curious savage offering to be Bud's personal guide to this way-off world at war. This man looked like Bud thought an Indian should. While there were no feathers, and he was the only one without war paint, he was wearing some buckskin and a few beads around his neck. He was not fighting like the other Indians, but was peaceful and acting like he wanted to explain to Bud what all the conflict was about. He seemed to care deeply for the boy, naturally upset by his confusion and fear.

Finally, with the terrible noises subsiding, the Indian introduced himself again to the amazed boy. Although they had briefly encountered each other before in this very place, it had never been this close and personal, and certainly not in the middle of an awful crisis. He came close to Bud and began to speak. When he spoke, the chaos quieted and Bud could hear him clearly. The Indian was anxious to share.

"My mother gave me my name, son. I told you when we first met. It's StarWalker. She chose it because she believed that one day the Great Spirit would allow me to move freely among the stars. She meant that my spirit would live on for endless moons after my body was done living. I would see many things and be able to share my wisdom whenever I could find a kindred spirit who would listen. You are such a spirit, little Bud, and I am here for you, today and any day that you really need me. And I'm here on behalf of many others, those noble souls whose bodies are now dead, but whose voices still want to speak and be understood and not forgotten. Please, Bud, don't be afraid of this dreadful fighting. It's ending now. I'll explain everything to you."

Bud's response was a mixture of wide-eyed marvel and feared madness. His mom was near the edge, at least according to village rumors. Was her problem catching? Had he moved from chicken pox to actual insanity? Or was he actually an especially fortunate young man?

"This is amazing! It's unbelievable! Am I crazy or something? I so wanted you to come to me again!"

"Yes, it surely is amazing, and no, you're not crazy. You are with me in Morning Glen where you should be, where the terror of yesterday's storm looks for a sunrise of hope, if not for itself, then at least for you."

With this bit of reassurance, Bud made an important decision. He would not run to his bike for a quick getaway, but yield willingly to the marvel of this haunting presence. It didn't matter whether the sound of this man's voice was going into his ears from outside himself or coming out of his own delusions from somewhere deep inside. The important thing was that the fighting was stopping, he was not alone, and he was beginning to hear important things. StarWalker certainly had a soothing voice. He seemed to be a caring old man who knew the world as no one else did.

"You and I are much alike, little Bud. I once was a tiny boy facing great sorrows. I learned that there is always hope, even when I couldn't see it at first. There's a big lesson here for you. Listen carefully." Bud surely was listening, and not sure if he could make his legs work even if he decided to run. StarWalker kept talking.

"You must rise above the blindness of most people, little Bud, a stupidity that reduces some to animals to be taunted while the dominant people rule the roost. You must learn to see what is not yet visible. For instance, you must believe in me even though others would think you strange and still fevered from your recent illness."

"I want to believe in you, Mr. StarWalker. But should I be afraid of you? I'm afraid of lots of things. I'm afraid of this awful war thing I'm seeing. I'm afraid of Mike Jakas at school and people who make people with black skin less than people. I'm afraid of what might happen to Mom, and even to Dad. I'm just afraid!"

"What you should fear, my son, is evil and ignorance, a blindness that can see only the moment, an arrogance that tries to subdue whatever is different, a blankness that fears what is merely passing by and then is gone." Bud was surprised by the reference to his recent illness and managed to break into StarWalker's lecture on wisdom.

"How did you know I'd been sick? Do you come out of the woods and watch my house at night or something?"

"No, little Bud, I just know. And I know that your very name calls to me and I must share your times of fear so that hope will flower for you again. Life can burst with new blooms, and right from what now looks like nothing but the dead petals of a poisoned plant. My destiny is to bring encouragement to you, my son."

"Are there poisoned plants here in the clearing that I don't know about? Should I be getting out of here?"

"Your former sickness has passed, little Bud, and there are no poison plants to worry about. And another thing. You keep wondering about whether I'm real. Well, yes, I'm real in my own special way, more real in the long run than most things. So much that now is real remains so only briefly and is soon be gone."

That comment about soon being gone was truly frightening to Bud. Was this old fellow saying that something is going to happen to Lucky or, worse yet, to his mom or dad? Who or what would soon be gone? But before he could get the courage to ask what the comment meant, Star-Walker had moved on to the subject screaming most loudly for his attention.

"By the way, my young friend, you'll notice that the fighting has stopped. Do you really want to know what all that Indian horror was about?"

"Yes! Explain it to me, and also keep me from getting hurt if it starts again. Do they have atomic bombs? There's not a desk out here for me to get under!"

"I can explain, and I will, and they don't have bombs. They lived and died long before such things existed. This war was actually a very long time ago. I know it's confusing, but I'll explain."

Finally, Bud's body was relaxing a little. He tried to fold his legs on the ground the way StarWalker had his. This was no ordinary school room. This was one of the few times that Bud had been in a class where the teacher had his full attention—and the lesson wasn't over yet.

"The Erie Nation was mostly peaceful, Bud, primarily hunters and farmers. Then in 1653 the Six Nations began to move westward from their traditional homes in Pennsylvania and New York. The English and Dutch colonists from Europe were in this place that they were calling "the new world." They were crowding the Indians, squeezing their hunting grounds, pushing them toward the western wilderness out here in Ohio. The colonists gave the Iroquois guns to help them conquer whatever they needed to once safely away from the white settlers."

"When? 1653? That's even before my parents were born!" StarWalker smiled in agreement and continued.

"One tribe that soon was conquered, my own, had become enemies of the Six Nations to the east. The reasons are not important now. They called us *Erielhonan*, "Erie" for short, an Iroquois word meaning "long tail." The French people called us *Nation du Chat* ("cat nation"), the long-tailed cats. Well, they sure did proceed to cut off our tails! And now you've seen and heard a little of the process and our pain."

Bud was stunned by this past conflict that now seemed so frighteningly near and present. His own problems at home and school seemed like nothing. Maybe that was part of the lesson he was to be learning. Star-Walker kept explaining.

"By 1656 we were finished. When Europeans first explored this Ohio area in the 1670s, none of us were to be found. We were dead or had fled elsewhere. You may be the first person in a very long time to glimpse our reality and understand how awful it was. We are glad that you know, and hope you are the wiser in your own life for knowing."

"Yea, maybe, I'm not sure." Bud wondered what Mike Jakas would do if a gang of bigger bullies dragged him off the school bus and beat him to a pulp. It surely was his turn.

"We had only bows and arrows, no match for the guns, so we were forced west of the Mississippi River, leaving around here virtually no permanent residents for a hundred years. Various tribes eventually came to wander through this Mahoning Valley, tribes with names like Miami,

Mingo, Chippewa, and Wyandotte—but no Erie, even though the big lake to our north now carries our name."

Bud had heard of Lake Erie on the radio lots of times. That's where the Cleveland Indians played baseball. Now he wondered for the first time what tribe that team came from. Were they named after SkyWalker's people, or just after Indians in general? Bud's mouth was hanging open. Finally, he managed to get a question formed into words and find the breath to get it out.

"But who are you? You're an Erie, you say, and you also claim that there were no survivors. How did you escape all this death and then manage to live for so long? Are you really alive? Am I crazy? How old are you?"

"Yes, I escaped, and I am old, really old. I know you have obvious questions; some things are so hard to understand. Fact is, I didn't escape the suffering—I always suffer with my people, but my spirit is now joined with that of the Great Spirit. Time is no longer an enemy of mine. I remember yesterday so clearly. I always hear the crying voices of my brothers and my children. I worked for peace, but many had other ideas—and still do. I'm still working for peace, maybe now in your heart, little Bud, and in your equally troubled world. I want you to know that enduring the pain of others can bring wisdom and healing for your own pain."

Bud's mind suddenly darted out of Morning Glen. He was grasping for connections and meaning that made sense for his own life. His neighbor, Hazel Halstead, liked to quote the Bible, especially in ways that supported her views. She was talking to Bud once and quoted some lines from Romans 8, justifying to the little boy her watching that evangelist named Graham on her TV. Then she came out with something that had stuck in Bud's head.

"Here's the thing, boy. Regardless of what my priest says about Graham being religiously dangerous, the Bible says this: 'You are not in the flesh; you are in the Spirit, since the Spirit of God dwells in you.... To set your mind on the Spirit is life and peace.' Graham says things like that too, so he's OK in my book!"

Bud sure wanted life and peace. He wondered at the time about the things Mrs. Halstead had said, but didn't dare ask her to explain more. Still, he now wanted to toss at her a flurry of questions. "Is this Spirit in the Bible the same as the 'Great Spirit' that StarWalker had just mentioned? Did Mrs. Halstead think StarWalker had been sent from God? How could she—I haven't even told her that he meets me here? If I asked her anything about any of this, would she tell everybody in the village the silly stuff that's on my mind? If she did that, and she probably would, Mike would hear somehow and the school bus would again become a hell on wheels!"

On the other hand, had he asked any of these questions, Mrs. Halstead might have been sympathetic, even helpful—she was a nice woman, after all, or she might have laughed and had great grist for her next bingo night splurge at the fellowship hall of her church. Bud couldn't know which, so he would not risk it—never ask, maybe never know.

StarWalker noticed the young man staring at him in wonderment—the fear was mostly gone now, but not the confusion over the Great Spirit, the ways to peace, dangerous preachers, talkative neighbors, nasty schoolmates, and dead Indians. Who wouldn't stare!

"Look here, Bud, I know your head's full of Mike Jakas, Mrs. Halstead, Rev. Graham, and lots of unanswered questions. Maybe this will help a little. Do you see this scar on my neck?" Bud dared to move close to StarWalker, almost close enough to smell him. He wanted to take a good look at the nasty gash that long ago had scarred over.

"How did you get that thing?"

"I survived the bad time of war, but not without my own pain and a lot of blood. Making peace isn't always easy or without danger. And, just like me, you can survive your bad time, Bud, especially with my help. I now walk among the stars, traverse the times, carry the voices and marks of yesterday, try to point to better tomorrows. I'm here for you. Together we can make it. You'll have to trust me."

StarWalker did something for the first time. He touched Bud, right on the side of his neck. He was gentle; even so, when his hand moved away, a little scar was there, a knife cut with the wound fully healed. It looked much like the one StarWalker had on his neck, just smaller. Was it, like StarWalker's, a sign of a battle once fought and a life that intended to prevail, no matter what? Shared pain has its consequences. When we care, really care, we carry each other's burdens, maybe even share each other's scars.

And then he was gone. Suddenly, it was just Bud and the trees and his bike and dog Lucky, and the little scar he didn't yet realize was now on his neck. The one remaining "long tail" had been severed from Bud's sight. So the boy rode home, hardly the same as when he had come to the clearing. When anyone in the future would notice the scar and call it to Bud's attention, he would dismiss it as an unfortunate result of the chicken pox. They had no way of knowing the truth, and wouldn't believe it if told. Bud had carried the pain of some others, if only briefly, and now he carried a sign of that sharing.

This marked young man would never forget the gentle touch of the old Indian, and he marveled now and then. That Indian war of long ago had actually touched even him. Maybe the past does impact the present. Maybe to know is to be different. To share is to be changed. How sad that few people ever get close enough to yesterday to have it change today for them. If only Bud could report his new knowledge to someone. But who would take him seriously? Those who have been among the stars hardly fit anymore among mere ground-walkers. You had to be there to really understand.

There was StarWalker, and now, in a way, there also was little Bud StarWalker, although he remained only Bud Kraemer to family and friends in the village. They didn't, they couldn't know. Sometimes he wasn't even sure he knew. Not even his mother understood, and she was the one who often dreamed of some escape for herself and maybe needed it the most.

Jessica certainly worried when she first saw Bud's little scar. She doubted that it was from the chicken pox, like he tried to say, but another source she couldn't imagine. She questioned Bud closely, insisting on an explanation that made sense. But how can anyone explain being marked by falling out of the present time and picking up the injuries of others from a distant yesterday? He didn't know how and didn't try.

"Mom, I didn't fall off my bike, honest, and no ruffians on the bus had flashed a knife at me." Then something truly frightening happened.

Bert came into the house and saw the neck scar for the first time. His reaction was sudden and very scary, a much bigger response than seemed called for. Bud saw in his dad's eyes genuine fear, almost like he'd been there himself, killing and being killed by the throat-slashing knives of the old Indians. Had the scar brought back to life some old battle of his dad's?

"Bud, let me be very clear. Never again do you play with knives or be around other kids who are—never, never! You were lucky this time, but in an instant one of those knives could shut you up forever—do you understand me, forever!" Bert said nothing else. Jessica thought he was on the edge of shaking as he went out back to fuss with something and mostly be alone and calm down. She and Bud were left wondering. She actually put her feelings into words, letting Bud hear them all.

"What was all that about? I've never seen him react so strongly to anything. Don't take it too hard, Bud. You shouldn't play with knives, of course, but you hardly deserved that kind of outburst. Try to forgive your dad—and do be more careful in the future. Please!"

"Well," Bud mused to himself, still waiting as patiently as possible in that nursing home, "that was all a long time ago. Now Dad just lies there, certainly not shaking, barely breathing. Back then I had no idea why he'd react like that to me and my knife scar. Now, having read those old letters of his, I have at least a beginning of an idea, and quite a new view of him altogether. So, please, Dad, please wake up for me! We didn't talk much back then, but I want to now! And you need to hear what I have to say."

Chapter Six

BINGO!

When a man's parent is dying, memories flood in and demand attention. Much was ending as Bert lay there on his nursing home bed. Yesterday still needed unraveled so that tomorrow could proceed. Bud kept waiting, and remembering.

Everybody in the village of Craig Beach knew everybody else when Bud was growing up there. There weren't that many people and even fewer secrets. Turn signals weren't yet standard on most cars, but they wouldn't have been used anyway inside the village. Everybody knew in advance where everybody else was going! Few turns were surprises. With little else to do, keeping track of neighbors, news, and even rumors of news was a widespread hobby.

The Kraemers on Beach Lane had a party-line phone (almost everyone did who had phones at all). Their ring was three longs and three shorts. When it rang that special way, Bud had found it fun to be the first to pull the receiver off the hook. After a minute or so, he would hear several clicks as others, deciding that the conversation wasn't worth eavesdropping on anymore, hung up one after the other. Neighbors wanted to stay informed, and this was one good way!

When Bud had reached the eighth grade, still at the Pricetown school that went from first to eighth, he profited greatly from the instruction of Joan Mason. She taught English and had just started Bud's class working on a novel they had to read and then write a report on. What was the novel's message? What could students learn from it in relation to their own lives? It was the first novel for Bud and had the funny title of *Winesburg, Ohio.* She told the class that it was a classic that they might be able to identify with and learn from since it was about a small Ohio town. If "classic" meant being around for a long time, then Bud thought of it as a StarWalker kind of book. Maybe there had been a big battle in this Winesburg town.

Bud was doubtful that he'd really profit from this book, although he did notice that it was published in 1919, the year both of his parents were born—was that a sign or something? Then he started reading and changing his mind about it having any meaning for him. Miss Mason had said that the author used as a model his actual hometown, Clyde, Ohio, near Toledo. It had about 2,000 inhabitants, much bigger than Craig Beach. Even so, things seemed to fit rather well. Then Bud had a perverse thought. Maybe he could get a little expert help.

"Who knows most about Ohio history? StarWalker, of course! Maybe he'll help me with some writing ideas!" But could StarWalker even read, at least in English? He talked in English. Was that another good sign?

"Well, whatever, that Indian at least can sure remember! Maybe he also meets with some boy in a woods near Winesburg. Of course, Winesburg apparently wasn't a real place. But Clyde, Ohio, was, so that was close enough. Bud would try to get his old Indian friend to come again to him so that the big question could be asked. Would he help? This assignment had a deadline!

Miss Mason wanted creativity and an identification of thoughtful relevance of the book, and she had warned against plagiarism. Bud and most of the other students didn't know that word, so she had explained that it's copying work from another person. Well, that would be no problem, not for Bud and his big idea. His rationalizing bounced shamelessly along cleverly constructed lines.

"Nobody but me believes that StarWalker even exists, so how could I be blamed for copying his ideas and words when he supposedly doesn't have any?"

The more he read, the more Bud needed to talk to somebody. It wasn't just that he needed writing ideas. This little book was really beginning to bother him. Characters in it felt familiar, unnerving, too close for comfort, a slice of real Craig Beach life with just the names and places changed. Weird! The teacher wanted an essay on what each student could learn for her or his life from this story. Bud thought, "She'd sure be surprised about some of my fears at home!"

That fact was, however, that Miss Mason wouldn't have been all that surprised. She knew more about Bud's home situation than he realized, much more, maybe more than she should have known. While she rarely if ever did the phone tapping thing, bingo games in the village were great times to learn lots of things, even "confidential" things.

It was a big weekly event, cheap recreation and organized socializing. The bingo games were staged at the little Roman Catholic parish fellowship hall less than a mile down the road from the village center in the direction of Youngstown. In this village, the center wasn't far from the edges! Joan Mason and Sandra Norton, the local doctor's wife, were good friends. They showed up nearly every week and often accomplished more than playing the game. They talked and talked, each making sure that the other was fully caught up on everything about local life.

Joan was single and needed the weekly outing away from her students and lonely apartment. She and Sandra were both professional women, trained to handle facts with care. But education sometimes seems to go only skin deep, at least on bingo nights. Sandra certainly shouldn't have said anything, and her husband John definitely shouldn't have said anything in the first place. They all were well meaning and had talked a little out of turn before this game night. Once together as bingo buddies, Joan's getting filled in on the home life of one of her students proceeded seriously.

John Norton was the local physician, a general practitioner, as most doctors were at the time. Even though his office was six miles from Craig Beach in the direction of Youngstown, at a crossroads called North Jackson where the area high school was, most adults in the village had been his patients at one time or another. He was kind and a good listener, traits not possessed by every doctor. Jessica Kraemer was a regular in his office. She had her physical problems, some chronic, and they would take her there when she could arrange the transportation.

Once in the doctor's presence, however, Jessica would pour out her heart to him about things beyond physical complaints—at least he was one man who really acted like he cared, if only for ten minutes every third or fourth week. That was more than Bert managed most months. One day Jessica told John a personal secret.

"I have inherited quite a bit of money from my dad's estate. The funeral was over in Pennsylvania. Bert, you know, my husband, dutifully went along, but ignored all the related details. He barely knew the man and doesn't like wearing a tie and viewing somebody already dead—says he saw too much of that in the war. Well, anyway, doctor, he never asked anything about any possible estate coming to me, and I have never mentioned it to him. But, believe me, I got some real money!"

Dr. Norton now was informed about why Jessica had that key in her little hope chest at home. It opened a very full lock-box at the local bank. There's where Jessica kept her inherited "dream dollars" as she called them. If not for herself, at least the dream was for her Bud one day. It was a secret escape account, a final answer to the question that haunted her. She posed it to the doctor, like he might have some pill he could prescribe as an answer.

"How do we get out of here someday, out of this village, out of our dead-end existence? It's killing me slowly, body and soul!" Dr. Norton made no response to this money, soul, and escape business. He tried to focus things back on bodily complaints.

During another visit, Jessica dumped more personal stuff on Dr. Norton, the kind that pills and shots don't help. She'd earlier had him swear never to mention her private box at the bank. He had sworn and kept this secret, but soon he shared with his wife Sandra much of what Jessica had said on that next visit. He was looking for advice from a woman's point of view. He probably shouldn't have done this for reasons of professional ethics, but he did. He was sure that sharing with his wife was in Jessica's best interest.

"How do I help this woman, honey? I can't tell you everything, but I've said enough that you've got the general idea. What do you think? I suggested that she take an anti-depressant, but she refused. She's a good woman, but stressed and in big-time denial. Sometimes I fear for her very life, not necessarily from her chronic illnesses so much as from her own hands!"

"Wow! That's a sad bit of news. I'm not sure what I think, so give me a little time to mull it over. OK?" Sandra planned a little research, that is, sharing the news with only "appropriate" people and collecting ideas from the reactions of her most trusted friends. Bingo night was the best time. She dare not try it over the phone. Conversations were hardly secure on those party lines.

Sandra cared for hurting people, but her caring was not always kept private. She'd certainly talk to her teacher friend, Joan Mason, a bingo buddy who also knew Jessica, or at least her son Bud. Maybe together they could come up with something helpful. Anyway, if she had no medical ideas, Joan's just knowing might be able to help even more than John ever could. Helping the son at school might really help mom at home—apparently home was a big part of the problem in the first place.

The needed talking between the ladies happened at the next scheduled bingo game, doubling the fault of confidence breaking—first John's, now Sandra's. No matter. Doesn't love trump the usual rules of secret keeping? Apparently so. In this case, Joan had the Kraemer boy in her English class at school and might be a better teacher for him if she understood Jessica's situation and its likely impact on the boy. The atmosphere was as electric as anything ever got in the village.

"Bingo!" Hazel Halstead seemed to have more dumb luck. She also had a big voice and a mind of her own. She told people that the priest, a defensive older man, had warned her not to watch on TV that Baptist preacher, Billy Graham, because he was anti-Catholic and a media heretic. That was all Hazel had needed. She began watching Graham every time he was on the tube with one of those big revival crusades of his. She thought he was handsome and sounded just fine. After all, he was pushing Jesus and encouraged loving your neighbors. "Isn't that Christianity?"

Hazel tried to do exactly that, push Jesus forward and keep track of her neighbors, her own way of loving them. She sometimes bragged about her independent approach to television watching—and did it right where her priest might hear her! Wasn't she taking a big risk, either that she would be excommunicated from the church or at least have her TV stolen by loyal Roman disciples of Jesus and put in the parish where only Fulton J. Sheen or the pope's speeches could be watched? Maybe it was risky, her mouth that is, but so far no Catholic commandoes had hit her house on Beach Lane. And now that she'd won again—and with a "B-12," the same as a shot she got from Dr. Norton sometimes, and the very channel that broadcast the Graham preacher.

"It's a sign!" she blurted out. Apparently God was really on her side and had a sense of humor! Her winning this particular game helped to hurry up Sandra's pressing agenda. Having a winner signaled a ten-minute break for coffee, snacks, and random chatting across the hall before the next game began. Joan started getting an ear full almost immediately.

"Listen, Joan, you need to know some things about the Kraemers who live on Beach Lane, right across the street from Hazel and Frank Halstead. You know their boy, Bud."

"Yes, I know Bud, but what about him?"

"Well, it's like this. Keep in mind that this is not mere rumor--I have two good sources, Frank Halstead and Jessica Kraemer herself. They've both been patients of John recently and they've both been talking to him. Understand now, you are not to repeat any of this because it's all in the strictest confidence. OK?"

"Sure, Sandra, but is your sharing such information with me ethical? I warn my students about plagiarism when writing. Aren't there some rules for doctors?"

"Yeah, but not so much in this case. This is important and helps a family. Just listen. We're trying to help you help your student." Joan was still hesitant, but all ears nonetheless.

The local rule, at least in the church's bingo hall, was that everything shared was in the strictest confidence, to be repeated to no one else except those interested in the latest and hottest, and only then after making them promise to keep it to themselves and being clear that it was all for a good cause. That hole-filled rule eliminated nothing except maybe admitting one's own unfaithfulness to a spouse—surely not in this village, at least not this week! With a little alcohol served (allowed at the Catholic fellowship hall, but definitely not across the lake at Ed Sinclair's Baptist church), even this sordid sort of thing slipped occasionally.

"Listen, Joan, and I'll have to make this quick. Jessica is depressed, maybe taking pills John's trying to give her, or maybe refusing to take them. She's barely coping. Really, she's hardly making it these days. John's worried about her, especially after Frank stopped in just two days ago for his usual sugar check—you did know he has sugar?-- and reported some disturbing things about Jessica's husband, Bert, and a woman he's been seen talking to very privately at his little marina."

"Are you saying we have a possible suicide and family break-up in the works?"

"No, at least I don't think so. Well, sure, maybe. It's a scary thing, Sandra, let's admit it. Nothing really juicy has been reported in any detail, at least not yet, but this woman of Bert's has a nice boat and docks it on the south end of the lake somewhere. She's a free spirit who drifts into Bert's place for an occasional fill-up, and maybe not with gas only, we're not sure. It's only a rumor, of course, but facts often hide under the covers of innocent-enough rumors. Hey, Joan, please remember. Don't tell anybody that I even brought this up! It's a really sad business!"

"Sandra, you said that 'we're not sure.' Who's the 'we'?"

"All of us who are worried about this. I've hardly shared it with another soul, only with certain people who have a need to know and might know how to help. Anyway, back to my point. Frank Halstead went by the marina just last week to buy some pop. Those two, you know, Bert and Maggie Welch, they were sitting in the bait shop chatting about something, rather friendly like, probably while Jessica was sitting at home alone, crying about being an inadequate woman or she wouldn't be so alone, and likely refusing to take the pills that my husband says could keep her alive. And poor little Bud—caught somewhere in the middle. See why you need to know and do something?"

"I suppose I do, but it's pretty much rumor and speculation. I dare not take advantage of it prematurely."

"It's not necessarily premature. We can't let all this go because of a little uncertainty, and it's not that uncertain. It comes straight from Frank who really saw something. He felt like he was intruding on really personal stuff he'd bumped into accidentally, so he'd left the marina quickly, without being rude, got upset some—and that's why his sugar went sky high and he brought all this up to John."

"Listen, Joyce, here's what Frank said to my John. 'Hey, doc, doesn't trouble in the village that I know about tend to raise the sugar level in the blood, or at least the blood pressure?' He wanted John to check him while he kept chatting about the bad thing he'd seen at the marina. So, there it is, Joan; what do you think about all this?"

"Wow! You're saying that Mrs. Kraemer is a hurting woman, cornered, unfulfilled, neglected by a husband who may be seeing another woman, only *maybe*, and now needing to be medicated by your husband for depression, but she won't cooperate, and my student is caught in the middle and in trouble too? And Mr. Kraemer is a preoccupied man who works all the time and whose sensitivity to his family is seriously lacking—and he finds it easier to talk to other women, the ones—at least this Maggie one—who share his boating and fishing passion, and maybe more passion than that?"

"Yes, good, you've got the whole, sick picture, Joan. So what do you think about all this, and their son Bud, and what you should be doing at school to help him?"

"All of this might be helpful information, Sandra, but I'll have to be very careful in how I use it. It reads like a novel, which is made up and yet could still have a basis in truth. Now, thanks to you and your too-much-talking husband (don't tell him I said that since he's my doctor too!), I know more about that village household on Beach Lane than young Bud probably does."

Sandra smiled, knowing that the next game was about to begin and she'd done a great job sharing some inside stuff that could save lives.

She could see that Joan was really thinking about it all, which is all she could ask of her. Joan did say one thing.

"Ironically, come to think of it, I just gave Bud a book assignment. It's a novel that might stir up for him some personal pain and give me a chance to relate to him helpfully about his troubled young life. We'll see. Maybe I can help somehow. I'll try to stay alert to openings for conversation with him, maybe after he turns in his book report."

Joan was a caring teacher, and now she was armed with information—if accurate—that she hadn't asked for and yet might ignore at the peril of one of her students, and one of the better ones, too. She began to wonder about the many times she'd seen Bud and another of her students, Betsy, talking like two embattled victims of life trying to comfort each other. Word had gotten out at an earlier bingo game night that Betsy's dad was an abusive alcoholic.

Joan looked at Sandra, with tears in her eyes. "It's pathetic to think that people so young should need to huddle up to survive!" Joan's mind was now running in several directions at once. One direction was being glad she was single! Then her thoughts were cut short.

"Let's play bingo, folks!" That shout out from the game master meant that the break was over and Hazel would have another chance to win. By her side was Frank, sugar under control, ready to roll, and with no rumors unreported. Joan and Sandra both glanced over the crowd trying to spot the marina-visiting and apparently home-ruining woman. Maggie was known, of course, but not well, and she rarely did the bingo thing. As a Baptist, it was rumored, she had been "saved" from the sinfulness of all things that might be fun in any way.

It was known that Maggie was divorced and had some money (probably got it from her ex). She lived on the other side of the lake from the village where Bert and the marina were. Her former husband, according to local "wisdom," had linked up with another woman and escaped to Youngstown, likely to get away from a woman who, it now seemed pretty clear to him, shamelessly ran around with other men. So Maggie was a loyal Baptist with a great boat and an unhealthy interest in Bert Kraemer. It wasn't surprising that she avoided showing her face much these days. Bingo had been dropped from her calendar. Maybe she didn't have any nights free.

Everyone Joan and Sandra could see in the hall was familiar to them. Maggie had slipped through their fingers for this one night anyway. Jessica and Bert weren't Catholics either, didn't go out to church anywhere so far as anyone knew, not even to the Baptist church where Maggie went. And in this village how could they go anywhere without people knowing it? If they had any family recreation, they kept it close to home, or out at the marina, and that usually would leave Jessica out. It was hard to imagine her with a fishing pole in her hands. She just didn't seem the type. And Bud seemed much like his mom, enjoying being alone, or at least being alone most of the time out of necessity. Maybe he had friends in a dream world somewhere. That might be better than having none.

There was another rumor, one well worth passing around. Somebody said they'd actually seen Bud going into the woods with only his dog, and doing it rather often. They hoped nothing strange was going on there. Had anyone seen a stranger about? Might the boy be in danger, or maybe have gone bad under all the pressure? The possibilities were disturbing.

The Kraemers were known by everyone as good and hardworking people, just not that social, especially Bert—unless he was with someone who shared his interests more than Jessica apparently did. She didn't seem to have any close friends, or Bud either for that matter. He was known to be the target of bullies. The bus driver had revealed that to Sandra at the bingo games just three weeks ago. That was another worry. People cut off can get hurt and do very strange things!

Chapter Seven

FLEEING WESTWARD!

B ud was faithfully reading that novel Miss Mason had assigned his class. It had gotten rather interesting to him, and then increasingly disturbing. Armed with the new information from the bingo game conversation, Joan Mason could imagine that the novel's setting and plot might not sit well with a sensitive boy living in Craig Beach with a highly dysfunctional family. She noticed Bud's discomfort and looked for her chance to talk.

This Winesburg, Ohio, place in the novel was a made-up town, so Bud's teacher had said, but to Bud it seemed so much like real life in his little village, and even in his own home. Hazel Halstead, his Catholic neighbor, told him once about the local bingo games. She liked them and thought they were good for the community. At least they got people out of their confining little houses and made a place where "news" could spread freely. That kind of simple game and candid socializing wasn't for the Kraemer family, however.

Bud's mother and father just didn't do the bingo business. If they had, it wouldn't have worked for Bud since his teacher was usually there. He had no idea if she went or not, but he couldn't show up when he was supposed to be doing homework for her and, if he went and she weren't there, somebody would tell her. It didn't matter anyway. He didn't have the money to play gambling games and his mother told him that gambling was wrong, as was the alcohol they served there.

Whatever research Bud needed for his paper would have to be done in the only place he knew. Since the nearest library was way off in Newton Falls, and it was a little one anyway, he would carry his book, paper, and pencil off to Morning Glen. Maybe there he could get some ideas for writing his report. Maybe StarWalker would show up and help him somehow. He wondered about the rightness of that idea, but had now justified it in his mind.

"If I get help from an old Indian, would that count as plagiarism in Miss Mason's eyes? I don't want to cheat, not like some of the other kids." He decided that it probably would be OK since it would all be by word of mouth, and from a "primary source" (the teacher said that was actually best), and from a mouth that people thought didn't exist! How could one track that and call it wrong? The Indian did show up, seemed to sense the situation, and began telling Bud another story.

"Little Bud, life often comes down to a simple question. Should we leave or not? George, the young man in this book of yours, had to face this question, and so did Clarence and Abigail Hutchins a long time ago. Listen to their story. It might help you with your assignment. Here goes. The story starts with Mr. Hutchins speaking."

"But I want to stay!" Clarence had been determined not to leave his Connecticut home. StarWalker went on with an explanation as he and the boy sat comfortably in the grass and leaned against neighboring trees just beyond the reach of Beach Lane. Lucky was there as usual, curled up nearest to StarWalker. Dogs know if things are safe or not.

"Clarence was at least willing to listen to Abigail's pleading that they really should leave or their lives might soon be over. His wife was wise and very insistent."

"No, my dear, we just can't stay, we can't! I want freedom from them Redcoats too, but it's the lives of our children that are at stake here. Those British soldiers are sure that you are the one who organized the meeting at the schoolhouse that got our neighbors so fired up for revolution. They're going to burn that place down as a lesson, and maybe even when our kids are there. They wouldn't care! We've got to go! There's open land out west and it's our best hope."

Bud finally was getting oriented to this story. They were back around 1775, just before the United States was born in the heat of revolution from England. He had no idea how this related to his book report, but StarWalker was on a roll and it might become clear soon.

"The schoolhouse was in Milton, Connecticut, a place that always missed the headlines. Unfortunately, it didn't always miss tragedy, and certainly not this time. It was an unincorporated village in Litchfield County, a little place seething with a longing for freedom from British tyranny. The real town nearby was Litchfield where once the leading minister was none other than Lyman Beecher and his family, including children Harriet Beecher Stowe and Henry Ward Beecher. But the near-by village of Milton lacked ample water and transportation to support industry, so it had become a sleepy backwater and later a little summer resort community, something like Lake Milton here. Now, with all the talk of revolution, it had become a place of great danger for the Hutchins family."

Bud was getting nervous, fearing that this story was about to yield more ugly Indian trouble and talk of more blood and death. He tried to stay calm.

"Clarence and Abigail lived near Milton with their four children, sur-viving on small-scale farming and fishing in the lake, and Clarence's on-and-off job in a clothing factory that could be reached in an hour on horseback—like your dad, Bud, and his truck going to the mills in Youngstown. They were the second generation of the Hutchins clan to live there and they were proud of their freedom in this New World. Cla-rence admitted to being a firebrand for the freedom of the colonists, but he also was a devoted Christian man who loved his family and wanted to be as sensible and safe as revolutionary. Being cautious and willing to flee wasn't an easy option for him. Nearly everything would have to be left behind; starting over would be difficult in the wild west."

Clarence was straightforward with his frightened wife. "Freedom is worth fighting for, even dying for, my dear Abigail! I'd risk it for myself without a second thought, and maybe for you too, but you may be right about the kids, especially Joanna."

"Why did she do it, Clarence? I told her not to get involved with that soldier. I think it was just the English accent and pretty uniform that se-duced her. Whatever it was, she let him do it to her and now he's ruined her life with one stupid, sinful night--and he could be the very one to set the schoolhouse on fire. That dapper Redcoat could turn our whole sky red and take our kids from us in a fiery hell!"

StarWalker stopped this scary story and motioned to Bud to come over next to him, sharing the solid support of the same tree trunk. He complied cautiously. Lucky shifted position, wanting to be close to both of them. Being this lose, Bud could smell the old Indian. It was a musty odder, gathered over the years by the clothes he might not change often. Then the old Indian touched Bud gently, sensing his anxiety. Bud saw again that ugly scar on his neck, but he hadn't noticed until now the red splotchy scaring on the back of his one hand. Had the old Indian been badly burned when he was young?

"It really happened, my son, the big fire in Connecticut I mean. Joanna got out alive, but not without some scaring, especially one ugly spot on the back of her hand that rarely could be covered from public view. She didn't lose the baby, fortunately, but the fire was more than the family could stand. Clarence and his family fled west, hoping to find their freedom in what came to be called Connecticut's 'western reserve'— right here in northeast Ohio. They settled in a little town where the stagecoach stopped regularly. It was called Fredericksburg. It was not far from right here in Craig Beach. It's mostly rotted away under water now, but it certainly wasn't then."

"Wow!" Bud's curiosity was really getting fired up—a lost city under the lake, his lake! A monster might be in the pond of Delores, but a whole city in the lake of Bud? And to think. Later, with the town gone, the lake that would swallow it would be called "Milton" like the tiny place in Connecticut. History has its ironic twists.

"Tell me more!" But StarWalker didn't want to talk more about that now. He had a big point to make and wouldn't be distracted from it.

"Back to your novel and the report you have to write, Bud. Those people in that Winesburg town of your book weren't real, you know, not exactly. That's the point of a novel. The made-up people are real in lots of places, only with different names but similar realities. Your teacher probably wants you to read the book and then look around you right here in Craig Beach. You need to let that book show you the presence of Winesburg on your own doorstep. If you once can see that, maybe you will be wiser in finding a way to deal with your school assignment—and even life as you know it. Clarence and Abigail Hutchins were real people of long ago who did what they decided they had to. You need to learn what you have to do."

Bud was now nervous because he was beginning to get StarWalker's point. He was squirming a little while Lucky was now fast asleep. Why does life come so easily to dogs?

"Listen carefully, Bud. Your mom and dad are real too, and really struggling, as you well know, and some day you too may have a big decision to make. You need to get ready for it. Someday you may need to leave. Your reason will not be British regulars, but you'll have your reason. Like I already told you, life often comes down to a single question. Should we (you) leave or not?"

Bud had closed his eyes, squeezing them shut with a rising tension as he heard about Joanna's tragic decision with that soldier, her close call with the fire, the family decision to flee west, and the idea that something like that may still be haunting the lake from somewhere down below, and maybe even stretching its slithering little fingers into the daily routines of his own family! Dare he write about any of this? He, of course, had no idea that his teacher was hoping he would. She knew that he needed to deal with some big things in his life and she wanted to help if he gave her a chance.

The thought of that burn scar on Joanna's hand shot a thought across Bud's mind that threatened to sear his very soul. StarWalker had the same kind of scar, and in about the same place! Was he in that schoolhouse fire? Was that possible?

Bud's eyes flew open, wanting another quick look to be sure his mind wasn't playing tricks on him. But he saw immediately that his friend was gone and he was now alone, leaning against a silent tree that had no comment on the minutes that had just passed. His memory was the only place to look—except for his own left hand.

He stared at it. It wasn't quite normal anymore. The pigment had been compromised. One spot in particular was like a quarter that was tarnished by years of use and stained a reddish color by something or someone. How had it gotten there? Could he wash it off? How would he explain it to his mother—his dad likely wouldn't notice, at least not at first. When he once did, given what happened before, Bud feared what he might do.

Bud kept leaning on the base of the tree, eyes closed again, stunned, truly scared now, his mind full of images—Redcoats, a school on fire, a lost city, people having to run away to survive, a burn mark on Star-Walker's hand, and now one on his too. And there were the sad people of Winesburg, and maybe even those of Craig Beach. Bud was swimming in questions. The new problem was that StarWalker wasn't there anymore to help with the answers. It was uncomfortably quiet in Morning Glen, but still all turmoil inside Bud.

"Oh, Mom, why do you cry so much? Do you want to leave Craig Beach, even Dad? Why? Where would you go? Could I go with you? Will I have to leave our village some day? Do we have any money we could use to live? What's in that little chest of yours I sometimes see you handling gently and then hiding? Does Dad know about it? Should he? Am I in trouble because I do? Is something bad coming? Will I be left all alone? Should we be running before something terrible happens?"

Then Bud tried to connect StarWalker's story to his own family in Craig Beach, even to the Winesburg place and people—after all, that was his assignment. The connection attempt came out as another series of painful questions for which he had no answers.

"Am I Joanna of Connecticut, or even George in my book? Have I done something really bad that could ruin our whole family? Is it my fault that Dad and Mom act the way they do? Did Clarence attack those British soldiers in anger and cause them to burn the school, and never tell Abigail? Had his own father secretly done something that none of them knew about? And what about a frontier town out west, not Winesburg or Craig Beach, but a Fredericksburg? Did the Hutchins family start over there, living with pain and secrets from the past that kept crippling their presents? Did they ever get away from there before they destroyed themselves, or had they found a place safe from all future running? Where would such a safe place be for him?"

Bud was a bundle of fears and criss-crossing stories. Unfortunately, this problem seemed to run in his family. He wanted to run away. But run where? Run away from the turmoil in his soul. But where can a young man go to get that done? Dare he write honestly, candidly, for his school book report? What would the truth sound like to his teacher? Could he trust what StarWalker had said? What really was the truth?

Chapter Eight

BREAKFAST INDIGESTION

B ud had gotten home and into bed without anyone noticing the new problem on his hand. He feared sleep because it might bring upsetting dreams. Then it happened, sometime near morning.

"It's a fire!!" The voice was Jessica's. Bud's heart was suddenly pounding wildly. The siren shocked the whole family out of a deep sleep. Her voice sent Bud into a brief panic, while the siren had launched Bert into a fast but very controlled set of pre-planned actions.

A crisis like this tends to jerk forward certain memories—and, they say, sends your whole life before your eyes with amazing speed. Bud lurched in his bed, already remembering Abigail and her family running from the big fire out east. Every member of the Hutchins family was suddenly a refugee fleeing to Ohio. Were they just now getting here? Were they now running up Beach Lane right now, looking for somewhere safe from the Redcoats who were still in hot pursuit? Had the Connecticut thing really happened? Was it just last night? Was it still happening? Would Miss Mason accept Bud's paper if he wrote about what had and was still happening? Would Mike Jakas find out that he was having American history delusions in the woods and in bed and laugh him clear off the school bus?

The siren was screaming from the roof of the village firehouse. Fortunately, it rarely came alive like this, but when it did it was truly frightening! Bud lurched up in his bed mumbling in frantic confusion, trying to get straight which state he was in, if Abigail was OK, whether it was Clarence and Joanna fleeing or the Russians who were coming with their big bomb. His mouth was on automatic.

"Is it the big bomb, Mom? No, it's the British! She shouldn't have done it. Abigail's parents tried to tell Joanna. Now they'll burn everything in Craig Beach too. Run west! Run west! Come on Clarence, it's our only chance! How did they get to Ohio this fast?"

Within seconds Jessica was at his side, knowing he was scared by the siren and assuming that he had been having a nightmare.

"It's OK, honey! You were having a bad dream. Yes, there's a fire and your dad's almost got his clothes on. But it's not our house and there are no British around here, and you're not going to have to run in any direction. You were talking about a Joanna woman, but I don't know any Joanna. I'm sure she's safe too—if she exists."

Bert was now jumping into his truck and Bud was out of bed and in his mother's arms. Jessica was trying to stay calm and help her son do the same. There was no way of knowing where the fire was, but at least it wasn't their house, and they could see out the windows that it wasn't a neighbor's either.

"This'll probably make your school bus late today, Bud, so get back in bed and I'll be close by until I can get a neighbor to come and sit with you. Then I'll go over to the firehouse to do my little job with the coffee for the men. We'll all be fine, trust me, and trust the good work of your dad and the others. They'll handle whatever it is. Your dad is really good at this sort of thing."

Bert was one of about fifteen volunteer firefighters who lived in the village. The siren was probably sounded by whoever saw the fire first, got to the station, grabbed the key that they all knew about, rushed inside and tripped the switch, and then tried to get the truck started before others began arriving. Since they never knew how many would show up, the rule was that when at least four of them were there they would go. Any others coming would soon get to the scene and follow the sights, smells, or sounds to the fire scene. The village wasn't a big place and fire had little chance of hiding.

Jessica was right. Bert was at his best in a crisis—he'd learned that during the war when there were daily drills on his ship. Men were to run as they dressed and be ready for action as soon as they reached their assigned stations. On this chilly morning in Craig Beach, he hadn't been the one to first see the fire, but he was man number two on the truck.

Man number one was Sam, the school bus driver. He would get to the kids today as soon as he could. Some things have to come before learning. One is survival for someone.

Sam yelled. "It's at the park, Bert! Here come two more guys—so let's go!" The truck was an old-timer, but the engine started right off and the men always kept lots of water in its big belly. It was a pumper that could handle most anything local—everything was one-storey and rather close by. If they ran out of water and were lucky, the fire would be close enough to the lake that they could easily get more.

They were on the scene of the fire in less than ten minutes after the siren had first sounded, despite everyone having been in bed. Well, not everyone. Frank Halstead couldn't sleep that night and had been wandering down Beach Lane in the moonlight toward the park. He's the one who had seen the flames and run to the fire station to set off the siren. Fortunately, it was as early as it was. An hour later and many of the men would have gone to work, some like Bert clear to Youngstown. In that case, whatever had ignited would likely have to run its full and tragic course. This time, however, the park was lucky. The fire was in the back of the bowling alley, probably from cigarettes the pin-setters had sneaked back there where the wood was old, even rotten. The place was full of smoke, but not many flames. By the time the men had dragged a hose down one of the lanes and gunned the truck's engine for a big blast of water that likely would have ruined the polished wood of the lanes, Bert was yelling.

"Don't bother, boys! It's already out!" Several of the old boards had burned, fallen away from the main building, and basically exhausted themselves, creating much more smoke than real danger. Bert had on heavy gloves, so he grabbed one board still red-hot on one end and tossed it into the little pond back there. There was a big sizzling sound, some steam rising from the surface, and then nothing but a little discoloration on the surface. Anything else that appeared hot was cleared away from the building to cool harmlessly. The windows in the back were opened so the smoke could get out and the men could be sure there was no more live fire anywhere.

Delores saw it all from her bedroom window. What a seat for the big show! Word would be out among the kids on the bus later that the pond monster had either started the fire with a hot blast from its nostrils or had eaten the fire for breakfast, saving the whole village! A third story, one that Bud would start himself, would be that Bert Kraemer had killed the dragon with his bare hands, burning off its head with a fiery board! Bud was proud of his father's courage in a time of crisis, but he'd have to be very careful about any dramatic stories. Sam, the bus driver, had actually been on the truck and probably wouldn't support any dragon theory he heard a kid expounding. If some beast tale were spun, Mike would leap on any such stupidity, especially if he found out that Bud had anything to do with it.

Delores would be sure that all versions were wrong. Yes, there certainly was a foot-biting dragon in that pond, she was convinced of it. What had really happened was that the dark-lagoon beast had swallowed a live fire-stick thrown by Bert Kraemer in a fit of anti-animal fury and was madder and more dangerous than ever! It had been no nice breakfast for the thing; the awful result was a belly-inflaming indigestion that the locals would soon pay for big time! Mike would think that just as stupid too, but he probably would ignore it because he liked Delores and would let her get away with stupidity. Bud sure hoped Delores was smart enough to not like him back.

Only minutes after the truck had roared out of its inside parking spot, the rest of the non-truck emergency crew had been on duty. Joyce Sinclair was at the fire station setting up a table of food from their store. That was the traditional thing for the boys when they got back, dirty, tired, and ready to eat. As soon as the neighbor had hurried over to keep an eye on Bud, Jessica had gone on foot the six blocks to the station— Bert, of course, had taken the pick-up, their only vehicle. Her job was the coffee urn. First, it had to be washed out after sitting there since the last fire or election day (the village voting was done here too), then filled with water and coffee grounds and gotten really hot.

Dr. Norton drove in with his black bag just in case one of the men got hurt—or some excited person knocked over Jessica's urn of hot coffee and burned feet. Maggie Welch was there to clean up. She might avoid bingo games, but a community-minded helper she was. She gladly would serve as needed and, given the rumors about her, probably would worry about Bert's well being. Like Dr. Norton, it took her longer to arrive from across the lake, so they didn't depend on her to set up or serve. Jessica was glad about that. The less she had to be around Maggie the better. She had heard the rumors and feared they might be true.

Hazel Halstead was the self-appointed "emergency communications officer," a title she made up and carried with great pride. She'd gather all the exciting news, package it to the best advantage of the village and herself, and get ready to share everything on the next bingo night and to a reporter for the weekly newspaper in Newton Falls. Hazel had already done some packaging of this one.

"My Frank was the hero who found the fire and set off the alarm that saved the whole village from disaster. And I know why the fire happened. God has judged his wayward children!" She was trying to be sure that everyone in the fire station heard her. This was really important.

"I can see that it's at the park—probably kids and cigarettes. Mr. Graham on TV says that God's judgment is coming soon—and I know it'll be by fire this time, not flood, a little one now in the village and soon the big and everlasting one in the whole world! So, dear God, protect our men in danger, and judge severely the young who have no standards anymore and endanger others with their terrible habits."

Joyce just rolled her eyes. She'd heard more than enough and said right out loud what was on her mind.

"Would they actually print stuff like that, Hazel? To be frank with you, I don't think it's worth the ink they'd have to use!" Joyce was a pastor's wife and knew something about the Bible, and she had a moderate dose of good sense. And she wasn't willing to allow this prophetic speech and off-base prayer to go unchallenged. With Hazel able to hear, Joyce continued aloud.

"Cigarettes are bad, sure, and my husband really doesn't like selling them at our store, especially to younger people. But if we don't, someone else will, we would lose valuable income and maybe have to close, and we all know who the someone else would be. Those kids would be going into Gerald's Tavern. After all, the people there sell all kinds of liquors and cigarettes and magazines, and to just about anybody. It's quite the problem, I tell you, and we wish we weren't involved with it at all. But at least Ed refuses to sell liquor and those magazines that have pictures of women who.... well, you know. There are lots of them right out in plain sight in Gerald's!"

Hazel knew the likely source of the cigarettes, if indeed that was the fire's cause. Was she meaning to suggest, even threatening to put in print, that Ed and Joyce were on their way to hell for how they conducted their village grocery business? Probably not, but it wasn't clear. Joyce held her tongue, mostly, saying as little as she could. Normally, Baptists had plenty to say about Roman Catholics, including straight from the pulpit, but not face-to-face and so personal like this. Maybe that's why Ed's congregation was on the opposite side of the lake and Gerald was a member in good standing of the Roman Catholic parish on this side—a delicate business in a small village! Joyce decided to speak directly to Hazel, being firm, but hoping not to make things worse than they already were. With the men seeming to have little problem with the park fire, she didn't want to start another one among the local women.

"Hazel, most of us have or at least once had husbands in the war. Maggie looked up, knowing the "once had" referred to her. They all seemed to pick up that bad smoking habit while away, and their kids have easily followed along. We're all copycats. Let's try to understand and be patient with the kids; we're all at fault in a way. Whatever's ruined at the park will probably get fixed soon, but our precious sons and daughters are a more complicated and way more valuable case. I think they have a better chance of turning out right in life if we are gentle and loving with them, not threatening them with damnation."

That brought some strained stares and some agreeing nods among the women, except for Hazel, that is. Such awkward talk ended suddenly when the fire truck drove back in. Within seconds it was clear that everyone was unhurt. It had not been a bad fire, one of those that could have lasted all morning and taken one of the men from his family forever, or maybe driven a whole family to the streets. Sam was the first heard speaking, and he wasn't happy, and his target wasn't the local smoking teenagers.

"We ought to make that Youngstown guy who owns the park pay for our time and trouble! Poor maintenance and lack of employee supervision is all it was!" Bert climbed off the truck and started pulling off his big boots and gloves. As she approached him, Jessica saw that one of the gloves was badly blackened.

"Are you OK, Honey? Is your hand burned? The glove looks awful!"

"No problem, Jess. I just grabbed a burning board and threw it into the pond behind the bowling alley. I'm not burned, except about the thing Sam's saying. I'm good and hot at that owner guy who should have kept this from happening in the first place. He likes our summer dollars out here, and takes as many of them as he can back to Youngstown. I don't mind him making a profit, but only when he's also being responsible with our safety. I say we send him a bill!"

Joyce heard Bert's comments and turned to Hazel. "There's the story for the paper, Hazel. Let's send a little damnation on the head of big-city irresponsibility!"

Jessica stayed out of that one. She was just so grateful that her husband was not harmed and that Maggie hadn't come over to check him out closely. Jessica so loved her Bert, despite everything. The problem anymore was that only in minutes of crisis like this fire thing did they really connect emotionally. It was so sad. It was so hard to understand.

Dr. Norton obviously wasn't needed, so he left quickly. He had patients waiting in his office. He knew that some of them were sick for about the same reason that probably caused this fire to be so likely, poor personal habits and bodily maintenance. His wife Sandra stayed behind and would help Joyce open Sinclairs as soon as they could. Sandra had her own car and was glad to help. The women's crew was needed to sooth nerves, fill the bellies of the tired men, and clean up before the firehouse got locked again, hopefully for a long time.

Sandra caught something sad out of the corner of her eye. Maggie walked over to the coffee urn and tried to express to Jessica her pleasure that Bert had avoided injury. What she got in return was a polite and suspicious smile. Nothing else was said. They were sharing a brief task, but certainly no trust, at least not on Jessica's part. She was happy that Maggie's role was the final clean-up. By then, Jessica and Bert would have gone home to get Bud off to school as soon as Sam could come with the bus. Bert would shower and be off to his regular work that paid real money.

More than the others, Sandra Norton realized how sad this little scene was. Jessica and Maggie, two hurting women, one divorced and the other feeling a little that way herself. One had risked some frank communication and had been rebuffed by the other, who now was hurrying away to be more private in her ongoing pain. Both cared deeply for Bert, one as her husband and the other as—well, who knew for sure?

Jessica did more than rebuff Maggie. She struggled quietly with her own husband—at least she still had one. She just couldn't understand Bert's response to an occasion like this. He had served well in what might have been a major village crisis, but then he wanted to go hurriedly his own way, avoiding the thanks people wanted to share. As always, he saw to it that his wife had no idea what his real problem was. She was never to know that he'd once gotten a war medal for a deed many called heroic but he classed as horrible. Sure, this village fire was quite a different thing, but his reaction to it was now a standard part of who he was. He'd carried the old pain of the medal incident deep inside for many years now, and it would remain there out of Jessica's sight. It was too horrible to ever share.

Bud was relieved after being reassured that there had been no angry British soldiers marching madly up Beach Lane to torch the Kraemer house. He didn't even try to explain to his mother that Clarence, Abigail, and Joanna had been real people driven off by fire, not merely a bad dream he'd had. Still, he was about to get on the bus and promptly get an ear full of strange tales of the morning's events, tales way stranger than the truth—unless one of them was actually true!

Some of the kids were hearing various things, all for the first time since their dads weren't firemen and they lived a little farther from the park and hadn't seen anything. Bud's only hope was that the angry dragon, according to some reports now struggling with severe indigestion from the swallowed burning board of Bert's, would not crawl onto land and travel around the village. If it did, it would be because it wanted revenge—especially hoping to get even with anyone carrying the name Kraemer. Bud knew his dad could take care of himself. What he didn't know, just like his mother didn't, was anything about a war incident that constantly haunted his father. Bert cared nothing about a monster in the pond; he carried his own inside!

There at least would be some good news on the bus. Mrs. Sinclair had sent out word that Bud and his friends were welcome to come to the store after school to collect a free ice cream cone—kind of a village victory party after the vanquished fire. Unfortunately, Bud had to consider such an invitation almost a threat. First, the store was close to the pond. Second, the kid on the bus making the announcement the loudest was Mike Jakas. If he'd be at the store for the cone distribution, Bud would skip the free treat. After all, the announcement had ended with a usual taunt.

"See you all there as quick as we can get away from the dumb school! And Bud," Mike had added, "do you hear me back there? I'm thinking of two cones for myself. I assume you won't mind if I eat yours too!"

Bud said nothing. What he was thinking was that there were two monsters in the village today. One had breakfast indigestion and was looking for revenge; the other was wearing boy's pants and riding on the bus!

Chapter Nine

I MIGHT DO IT AGAIN!

Sinclair's store delivered on the free ice cream. Even so, and despite how hot it was outside and how good it would have tasted, Bud made no appearance. Joyce noticed his absence, guessed why, and was thoughtful enough to call him afterwards. Bud was home, heard the three longs and three shorts, and answered.

"Bud, this is Mrs. Sinclair at the store. Your father did a great job for us this morning and I happen to have an extra cone down here, and it's free. And there's something else you need to know. Right now there is no one else is in the store right and I still have one cone left. Interested?"

"Thanks! Since no other kids are there, I'll be right down!" What he didn't think about was the party line and the possibility that Mike Jakas might have randomly picked up the call to see who wanted what with the Kraemer household. Fortunately, Mike hadn't heard the call this time.

Ed Sinclair did more than reluctantly sell cigarettes—and it was very reluctant. He kept them out of sight and people had to ask for them. He was also a Christian pastor and always closed his store on Sundays. Sometimes that gave him the freedom after the morning church service to come across the lake in the warm afternoon to visit his good friend

Bert Kraemer. Bert wasn't anti-social, not at all. Catch him at the marina and bring up a comfortable subject and he was downright talkative and pleasant.

Bert was mostly comfortable with Ed. Occasionally the pastor did have a bit of an agenda, but usually Bert could take that much. "Maybe," Ed would think as he crossed the lake, "my sermon of the day could be adapted to a good man who hadn't gone to church but needed the good news anyway." Bert always could be counted on to be at his marina on a weekend, ready to service boaters and fishermen, and glad to talk to Ed. Here was one religious guy who wasn't too pushy about his religion and also had some good tales to tell from back in the war years. For some reason, veterans didn't usually talk about war experiences with their family members, but they surely would with each other.

Ed's boat was modest in size and had only a small motor, nothing like the large and fast recreational boats cruising the lake on a nice day, especially on weekends. He was known to actually try rowing across the lake—nearly one mile--if he weren't in a hurry and the weather was good. When he did, it was quite a sight, a pastor after church, and with only one arm at that. He had to use the two oars alternately.

The boat wouldn't travel in quite a straight line or move very fast, but he managed surprisingly well. He'd sit in the middle of the seat and reach first to the left and then the right. If one of the motorboats flew past anywhere near, large waves would soon reach him and come close to swamping his boat. No matter. He did have a useful stump, and he was strong, proud, very proud, and knew the lake well. He'd get straightened out as necessary and keep going. If it got to be too much, he could always resort to the motor. Bert would see him coming and be happy for the visit.

Usually they would sit in the shade and talk about old times, especially the war. On this particular day, however, Ed had more on his mind and was not alone in his boat. Maggie Welch had come along. Ed decided to use the motor all the way, maybe because they had a serious agenda for this visit, and he wanted to get there more quickly and be less exhausted. She attended his church, appreciated his ministry and pastoral counsel, and really needed to talk to Bert.

The need didn't relate to the rumors about her and Bert. She tried to ignore them. Her former husband, Herb, had been on the same ship as Bert during the war and knew what had happened that so upset Bert. Sure, he had left Maggie, not able to settle down anymore, attracted by a younger woman from Youngstown. Some months before he left, however, he had told her what he assumed was the whole sad story. Bert now needed to be aware that she knew what had happened on the ship, and he needed to be strongly encouraged to finally face the truth that he was hiding. Here's what Herb had told her. She was about to repeat it to Bert as faithfully as she could remember the story.

There had been Japanese prisoners aboard the ship on which Bert and Herb had served. It happened one fateful night when Bert was on watch topside. One of the prisoners had gotten free below deck somehow. He had made it topside and began sneaking around on deck, desperate and threatening, looking for a weapon. His presence didn't get past Bert's notice despite the darkness. Bert recognized the danger to the ship and, without hesitating, got the prisoner from behind. The frantic figure on the shadowy deck resisted vigorously. So Bert used a knife, viciously killing the man--and then, two days later in a big ceremony on the same deck, he received the formal praise of his captain for heroic courage. Bert had done what was necessary, and what only he had a chance to do for the sake of all his grateful shipmates. That's what the citation said, and in flowery language.

Well, that was the dramatic war story that Maggie was about to announce she and Ed knew in detail. Ed's little boat finally reached one of Bert's marina docks. Three and a half arms were aboard, and the truth about yesterday was heavy on the minds of its two occupants. As it bumped and slid to a stop, Ed held the dock with his one hand while Maggie tied them off at the bow. Bert was there to see if they needed any gas or had just come for a visit. Bud was with him, loving the lake on a day like this, and the chance to be with his dad a little bit.

"No gas needed, only some good talk," said Ed. Once up in the marina itself, and on the only three plastic chairs that Bert had in the place, they exchanged routine pleasantries. Bud soon said he had to leave because his mom was expecting him for some home chores. As soon as he was out of sight, the real talk began.

Bud would have to decide whether or not to tell his mom that Maggie had come to visit his dad again. He decided to say nothing—what would be the point. It probably would cause his mom to worry more, maybe even cry again. And, after all, Pastor Ed was there too, so it must be all up-'n'-up. It was broad daylight, other boats were coming in to get gas now and then, and it all seemed perfectly innocent, despite what about everybody in the village knew Frank Halstead was reporting. In fact, it was innocent. Unknown to Bud, however it was quite serious. Maggie had started right in as soon as Bud was out of hearing range.

"Bert, Ed here preached this morning about the power of memories, the good ones we have about Jesus and the bad ones from our own lives that can ruin things for us. I wish you'd been there." Then she looked him right in the eyes, freezing him in place.

"My Herb, your old friend, Bert, told me all about it one day before he left me. He really admires you, knew all about what you did to that prisoner on the ship, and how much it still bothers you despite how other people honored you at the time." She could tell that Bert already had kicked into his standard denial mode.

"Are you sure Herb got that right, Maggie? He always could blow up the truth way bigger than life." Bert looked at her half teasingly as another part of his diversionary tactic. A cornered animal keeps dodging, useless or not. Before she could answer, he got in one more distracting jab.

"And something else. You can't always trust what a preacher puts into your head! Or communications officers either—you surely know what Hazel Halstead and her fast-talking Frank are saying these days about you and me. I guess I'm the first in village history to slay a dragon during a park fire and save the world all by myself, but just before many of us are going to be judged and sent to the lower region anyway for outrageous sins, like smoking (he did himself), or rowing a boat with only one arm, or meeting a secret lover by the lake in broad daylight!"

They all laughed, enjoying the pointless humor, and were glad for a little break in the tension. But Bert was merely ducking the painful truth. They all knew it, and Ed and Maggie hadn't come to let him get away with it again. Maggie chose to be very direct. No one had ever done this before with Bert.

"Bert, the rumors are just stupid, you and I know that, and this preacher friend of ours here can surprise you sometimes with gentle patience instead of roaring hell fire—and I think rowing with only one and a half arms is just wonderful! He and I know you're a great, hardworking, honest guy, but—counting Herb--at least three of us also know that the killing did happen and that it's still killing your personal and family life. And here's what Ed and I have to say about that, Bert. It's not necessary, not right, and your suffering and silence should stop!"

Bert hesitated, thought some, and then responded. This was painful stuff. He felt his life was on the line. He now was rigidly defensive.

"Can't do that, Maggie. Absolutely can't do that. And you and Ed are never to tell—never! You might mean well, and I'm sure you do, and I really appreciate that, but it makes no difference. Facts are facts. I don't want Jess to be afraid when I'm around—I try not to be too much. And I surely don't want my boy knowing that his dad's a brutal killer! I couldn't ever hold my head high again if they knew. Never do that to me!"

Listening to Maggie repeat this bit of secret history had frozen Bert inside. He stayed defensive and suddenly said, "I had him from behind just as I'd been trained to do. He had a weapon, was our enemy, and it was my duty, so I did it. I cut his throat in an instant!"

Now it was totally quiet in the marina. The air was so thick that it could have been cut itself. That's how Herb reported what happened. And now, with some extra detail, Bert was admitting it, at least to these two good friends, and for the first time in many years. What Herb didn't know, however, was the great fear that Bert still carried with him. It was paralyzing. Citation or not, applause and back slaps from his buddies or not, the ugly event of that killing was haunting Bert to this day. He had never said a word about this to Jess. Some nights he would dream, reliving those awful seconds. He felt sorrow, even shame, and dreaded one thing more than all else. He came right out with it. It was in the form of a terrible question.

"Here's the really big thing I don't know. Even if my family knew and could forgive me, might I be capable of doing something like that again, and even with less provocation? Could I ever actually hurt Jess if she expressed anger at my insensitivity, or resisted my way of disciplining Bud? Could I hurt Bud—like when he came home with that knife mark on his neck and I started shaking with fear? Am I now a violent man at heart? I have blood on my hands and the years have not washed it off!"

Bert volunteered one occasion when things had almost gotten out of hand. Once, in the midst of this nightmare, some words had just flown out of Bert's mouth, with Jessica right there. "Dear God, NO!!" is part of what came out. Jessica was shocked, awakened him, and asked what was wrong. Bert said only that it must have been a bad dream and really meant nothing. He was sorry for disturbing her and they should both try to get back to sleep. He would say no more.

"Alright," said Ed, "we hear your great fear. But try this out for size, and I mean this kindly, my friend. You say you would never be able to hold your head high again if your family knew the truth. Well, I don't see your head being held all that high right now! Man, can't you see that Jessica and Bud already know that something is wrong, very wrong, and that you just suffer and let them suffer, and even let Jessica imagine terrible things about you and Maggie that aren't true at all? The truth would be so much better—and you might be surprised at how your family would respond. We know, and we think no less of you. And they want so much to really know you. And once they did, they would love you even more, and finally know that you really love them too."

"Maybe, but only maybe, Ed. And if you're wrong, what then? It's too big a risk as I see it. No dice." After a pause, Bert's brow tightened a little.

"And about Jess thinking something wrong is going on between you and me, Maggie, are you suggesting that my family doesn't know that I love them and actually thinks that I'm being unfaithful?"

"Bert, I'm suggesting exactly that!"

Ed was also anxious to answer that question. Maybe Bert would hear him and do something differently. "Bert, your family is confused, very confused, and you make it hard for them to feel love from you. Worse yet, Jessica is quietly humiliated, believing that it's Maggie and you, secretly a loving couple behind her back, and she's the odd one out, not loved, a stray piece pushed off the puzzle table and hardly even missed!"

Bert just stared at his friends. "That's stupid! My Jess thinking like that? Is this whole village a smelly pond of silly rumors? I've never loved anyone but Jess! Where did you people get your information?"

Ed answered quickly. "Well, I've not talked to her behind your back if that's what you want to know. The strange way she and Bud act in public, or mostly by staying out of sight, and the constant rumors, those are my only sources, I admit. But remember that perceptions of reality are the reality for people who have them—and what we are saying is the common perception in this village."

"No matter, Ed, it doesn't make any difference. As I said, I can't take the chance."

"But Ed's right, Bert," pleaded Maggie. "You can keep digging in your heels, and you're probably the most faithful spouse in the village. That's likely God's complete truth, and I ought to know, but whatever your wife believes is the real truth to her—and, Bert, you choose to allow her to believe the wrong thing day after day. You decide to let her think a lie. And your boy thinks you're OK with his being upset and even humiliated much of the time in front of his friends."

Bert absorbed this heavy hit and looked blankly across the lake, saying nothing, and maybe numb enough that he was thinking nothing—who knew? Here were good friends saying very hard things, and as gently as they could, and he knew they were right.

The spell was broken by a big boat arriving at the dock next to Ed's and calling for Bert's immediate attention. It was a silly scene, a lovely cabin cruiser all set up to pull water skiers and needing more gas, snuggling in next to a little fishing boat with a ten-horse motor hung over the back and sometimes replaced by the sweat power of a one-armed man!

Bert was actually glad that it had come. He needed the sun and some fresh air. The inside of his marina had suddenly gotten too hot for comfort. Ed and Maggie were dear friends, sure, but they were asking for more than he could make himself give.

When Bert finally came back inside, Ed and Maggie had helped themselves to cold pops, with their money lying on the counter. Maggie took a good drink and then spoke first.

"So, Bert, we're done. No need to repeat all this again. But here's my question. Do you want to take this ship secret to your grave, and let your family take all their hurt and confusion to theirs? Is that it, my friend?"

He just stared at her, finally saying, "Nope, I sure don't want that, and you know it, Maggie, but I haven't the nerve to do anything else. I admit it, OK? I admit it. I'm a wonderful example of the strong and independent man who doesn't have the nerve! Does that little confession make you two feel better? I'm trapped like a fish on a hook, like lots of other people in this village. It's a lovely place to play and live, but it's full of frustrated residents with checkered pasts. I'm trying to make the best of mine. My past is poison for my present, I can see that, and I guess I'll have to keep drinking it, even if it kills me!" Bert then added a religious barb, a sharp question to which he expected no answer.

"Why doesn't your God fix this thing, Ed?" Ed kicked into his pastor mode, and not too defensively despite the emotion. He loved Bert, but had no intention of backing off completely.

"God's trying hard, Bert, but you'll have to cooperate. He'll not violate you by forcing you against your stubborn will."

"I'm glad about that—I'd fight any forcing! My will has kept me afloat all this time." Ed smiled, well aware of Bert's strong will. He added only this.

"By the way, here's something more to think about, Bert. Have you noticed that just today God's been working on this? He sent you two loving servants of his, not perfect angels for sure, but at least well-meaning people who've come to see if they could help you find your way with God's help. I'm sorry to report that so far they haven't made much headway."

Bert turned away. He had a pencil in his hand from the last gas transaction. Suddenly, he threw it violently against a wall of fishing gear, knocking off a bobber that hit the floor and smashed.

"Damn that Jap! Why didn't he stay locked up where he belonged, or at least have run into some other guy who would have killed him and promptly forgotten about it in the flood of congratulations? But, no, it had to be me, and I did it, and it won't go away!!"

Now Maggie was crying, even scared. She spoke to Bert as gently as she could.

"I know it really hurts, Bert, and we're hurting with you. Still, Jessica is having a really tough time of it too, and Bud sometimes acts like a pretty unstable young man without a dad. You're the only one who can help them. You took a life once because you had to—and, scared or not, it was right in front of you and you did it without calculating the possible costs to your reputation. Now you have a chance to save a life, maybe two or three. Please, Bert, do it, dare to do it without first calculating the costs."

Somebody hollered up from a dock, ending the drama that wasn't going anywhere anyway. "Got any fresh worms today? I'll take two dozen." Bert sure did and was glad for the change of subject.

Chapter Ten

DEEP LIKE THE RIVERS

"Dive! Dive!" Friends were encouraging young Bud Kraemer to go head first off the dock into the lake. He loved the water, but the head-first thing was just too much. He was anxious about lots of things, but especially about something under the water he couldn't see. One mistake and no more head! He just couldn't commit like that and not be able to stop what might be a deadly plunge.

As a boy, swimming was so much fun for Bud, as was helping his dad sell worms or hooks and listen to fish stories at the marina. Bert wasn't always in a lighthearted and storytelling mood, but occasionally he was. This was the best way Bud had to connect with his father, a mill man who didn't much appreciate his love of books and attempts at poetic or abstract thought. Don't misunderstand, Bert was quite intelligent and did love his boy, especially when Bud was being practical and had his hands constructively dirty. For some reason that Bud couldn't comprehend, however, his dad avoided thinking whenever he could—or at least sharing whatever his thoughts really were. He wore masks to protect himself from an unseen enemy.

What worried Bud's mom was less the chance of drowning and more the boy's many trips and occasional long stays in that little clearing down the street and into the woods—or so he told her. Was something wrong? Jessica had begun to really worry about her Bud. He was fast becoming a young man—and he was so important to her! Was she losing him? She couldn't bear the thought, not both Bert and Bud!

It was fine with her that Bud was more gentle-natured and reflective than the other boys in the neighborhood. She was like that too. But some of his comments were just too different. Once he had said something about a Mr. StarWalker and Six Nations fighting a long time ago—and he claimed that he knew this old Indian and was there personally for the fighting! He even claimed he'd been part of a fire out east in Connecticut in the 1700s—and supposedly now there was a hidden Fredericksburg city under Lake Milton. Really? That would stretch the mind of anyone. So Jessica finally confronted him one day.

"I've got to know the truth, Bud. What's really going on with you? Where do you really go? Are there older guys out there smoking cigarettes or maybe drinking alcohol? Are there girls out there? What?"

"It's just a little clearing in the woods, Mom. I go there alone lots 'cause it's quiet and I can think—and there are no other boys or girls out there, although sometimes an old man comes to visit me. There's nothing wrong with that. He's very nice and a real friend. He tells me stories and I love them. He won't hurt me, Mom, I'm sure. That's all. Honest, that's all."

Bert wasn't worried about the clearing stuff. He was too busy working at the mill and marina to bother about such kid business. Sure, Bud was a little different, not the tough-kid son he would have preferred, but how he was shouldn't be thought of as hurting anything. At least he hadn't picked up smoking, something that Bert would have tried to stop. But a fertile imagination, old Indians, lost worlds, whatever? There was no harm in such things, just no practical good. Bert wished that Bud were more hands-on and less inward about life, but that's as far as his thinking had ever gone. He was too preoccupied with the fears and denials of his own inward life. He'd never forget that recent visit of Ed and Maggie! He had refused to tell the truth, and made them promise never to breath a word of it.

Jessica, on the other hand, had lots of time to brood. She could imagine the worst and dreaded any more loss in her life. One day she'd had enough worry about Bud and the woods. It was time to find out the truth.

"Come on, Bud, we're walking down to the woods together. You show me this place of yours. I want to be sure it's nothing more than you say—and I want to meet this old man, if he exists."

"OK, Mom, but you're wasting your time. It's just a little grassy nothing. You'll probably get scratched getting in, maybe even touch some poison ivy, and you'll be sorry! And don't expect to meet my friend. He's only mine and usually not there. And he doesn't live anywhere around here. When he thinks I need him, he comes—and from very far away, and not when other people are around except me."

"That doesn't sound right, Bud, and I just don't like it. A stranger doesn't act like that unless something sinister is afoot."

Bud was sorry that his mother couldn't let it go. So they walked down Beach Lane quietly and together, with Lucky trailing along. She held his hand—he sure hoped nobody saw that or he'd get teased without mercy on the bus for being a mama's boy. She was genuinely worried, and he was a little hurt that she was suspicious and not trusting of his report. No matter, that's how it was. So they arrived and Jessica tried to avoid getting scratched—and she sure didn't want any poison ivy. Once in the clearing, she realized that Bud was right. There was nothing unusual to see. It appeared to be just a place for a boy's imagination to run a little wild.

Bud didn't know it, but she'd already talked to people who lived on that end of the village. Had they seen or heard anything odd? They had reported to her that no one had ever seen an old stranger lurking around. And when they sometimes saw Bud and his dog go into the woods, they hadn't heard anything out of the ordinary.

Well, that was that. Now that Jessica was satisfied, they walked back home. Once there, Jessica had some advice for her son. "Bud, listen, it's OK to pretend and make the best of being alone—I have to do that all the time it seems, but don't talk about it too much. People will think you're odd, and that makes you and the whole family look bad. You're special and I don't want you misunderstood or hurt." She didn't fully realize how late it was for that caution.

That's when Bud admitted to his mother that he was already getting hurt sometimes. After an example or two, they were both crying. Bud was less caring about family reputation than his mother and went on to explain something to her. It had to do with that Walden Pond business he had learned at school.

"I may be strange or odd, Mom, but there are people, important people who agree with me and act like me. For instance, there was a Thoreau fellow out east who thought like me, and he got to be famous— my teacher in Pricetown loves his writing and has us read some of it. Miss Mason said he believed that it doesn't matter what you look at. What matters is what you see."

"Well, Honey, your teacher is a good woman. I don't know Miss Mason very well, but I've seen her around and heard things, and she seems nice enough. And I can sort of understand what you're saying. Seeing what isn't there, at least for the one looking, makes it actually there in a way. I've never heard of Thoreau, but I do have a book about famous painters and sculptors. I've actually been reading it, Bud, partly because I've been worrying about you and trying so hard to understand you better." He smiled, realizing again how much she loved him. That felt so good.

"One man called Michelangelo—an old man from far away like your Indian friend--is supposed to have said that he saw an angel caught in a block of marble. So he carved away until it was freed—and the result was amazingly beautiful. And guess what? I can see "angel" right inside this sculpture's name. Maybe we should try to chop it out!"

They both laughed. Jessica could be funny, but these days only when she was relaxed and alone with her beloved Bud. Nor was she done with her little philosophy lesson from the arts. She was taking full advantage of having Bud's ear.

"And there's another man, a painter called Picasso. He's somebody who claims to paint objects as he thinks them, not as he sees them. That's interesting and certainly a little weird, but I guess for him it works or he wouldn't be famous. The fact is, Bud, that I've looked at pictures of some of his paintings and I don't get what he was thinking! Maybe I'm not supposed to, I don't know. There are lots of things about life I don't get, and apparently lots of life that I'll never have. I sure hope that's not how things are going to be for you!"

Bud smiled with appreciation for her deep caring. She showed him the book and the Picasso pages--he didn't get it either. He was comforted that his mom was really trying to relate to him at a deeper level and admitting that what some people called great art looked to both of them like a kid's first effort with messy finger paints! He knew that life wasn't easy for her. At least she was now sure that Morning Glen was just an ordinary clearing and the old Indian wasn't some runaway convict hiding in the woods and waiting to hold a boy for ransom. Since she wouldn't forbid him to go back there, he decided to risk telling her one other thing he had from school.

"Mom, I love you, and thanks for coming to my special place, and showing me the pictures, and trying to understand. Could I tell you another little quote the teacher gave us when we were talking about that Thoreau guy?"

"Sure, Honey, why not? Maybe you can convince me that a really old woman is waiting to visit me in a clearing next to yours. If she's also wise and passes out free tickets to Europe, I sure hope she becomes my special friend!" They were both smiling and dreaming a little.

"Here is it, Mom, and it's no old lady. Somebody once said that a rock pile is no longer just a rock pile once an architect looks at it carefully and sees it as building blocks for a cathedral. That's what Miss Mason said. Maybe I'm doing some special looking like that when I go to my clearing and see wonderful things in the most ordinary stuff. I don't have the cathedral yet, Mom, and I don't even know what one looks like for sure, but I've got a bunch of blocks to work with now, and I'm trying hard to build something good."

"Wow! I get that, Honey. I wish I saw all that you do in that little woods place, but maybe I just can't. In fact, I wish I saw more than I do here at home, day after day, boring task after meaningless task, but I don't. I only ask that you be careful, use good sense, and don't talk too much to people about your little flights of imagination. If people take you too seriously, it'll be plain embarrassing for the rest of us. I'm embarrassed enough as it is."

"What about Dad? Do you ever tell him the stuff you're telling me?" She suddenly got quiet, acting like she wanted to look away.

"Bud, I used to, lots, but not much anymore. I don't think he's interested." He thought he saw tears in her eyes. That ended their little talk on a quiet and sad note. When it came to Dad, there just wasn't much to say. He was like a machine, well oiled and efficient, but without much warmth and humanness.

That kind of frank talking with his mother wasn't as frequent as either she or Bud would have liked, but it was precious when it happened She worried about him, and he had begun worrying more and more about her. Bud was sure that she was quieter and even slower moving all the time. He was afraid that she wasn't eating right or was sick or something, but he didn't say anything. Maybe she would be embarrassed at not looking her best, and he didn't want any more of that for her. He wondered if his dad was noticing the same thing. Probably not.

Within weeks of that day of their special talking, all the fun stopped. Bud was right. Jessica had been losing weight, and for no good reason. Bert and Bud joined her in being really scared. Finally, Bert took the time—unusual—to get her to a doctor in Warren. These symptoms were beyond the testing ability of Dr. Norton's office, so he had referred them on. A doctor and some laboratory people did the necessary testing over there and then asked the Kraemers to come back in three days for the results. That was hard for Bert, who would have to take off work again, but he guessed there was no choice and did what he had to. What they were told changed everything.

"Cancer. Terminal. So sorry." The doctor was unnecessarily abrupt with his reporting—not like Dr. Norton would have been. This medical stranger acted nervous and in a hurry, and had nothing to suggest other than going home and staying as comfortable as possible. He'd send her home with some special pill that would help.

"Awful! Just plain awful!" That's all Bert said to the doctor. He looked tenderly at Jessica, but had no words for her. He just didn't have any. The reality was too big and bad, and too much of himself was stranded elsewhere.

"A few weeks or maybe months at most," that's what the doctor also said. In the car on the way home, Bert repeated out loud these fateful words. They made his insides feel like old jello rotted in his stomach and now wanting badly to hurry up or down to get out of him. He managed to get home without throwing it up. Jessica then went to bed with her pill. Bert sat in his chair and mostly stared at the walls. Bud came in and was told the sad news. He immediately knew what he had to do.

He grabbed his bike and rode to his secret place, crying all the way. He just happened to have one of his school books in the bike's little basket that was anchored to the handlebars. Once settled at the base of his favorite tree, he opened it up to a page recently studied at school. Something about some lines there seemed to offer a gleam of hope for a boy suddenly dropped into a pit of despair. It was from some church hymnal which said the lines were to be sung to an ancient Irish melody, with the words related to Psalm 119:105 from the Bible.

> Be Thou my Vision, O Lord of my heart;
> Nought be all else to me, save that Thou art—
> Thou my best thought, by day or by night,
> Waking or sleeping, Thy presence my light.

How Bud needed vision, a divine presence with him, light in the darkness that was fast crowding in on his whole life! He just sat there, looking blankly at an empty world.

The tree itself was at least a small encouragement. It was tall, straight and strong, unchanging. Very soon none of that would be true of his mom. Those music lyrics were kind of mystic, mysterious, almost magnetic. He needed all of that, and badly. His dad was upset, really upset, hardly even talking to his mom—and she really needed him to! Bert had plenty of feelings; it's just that he kept most of them buried somewhere inside him. Something blocked the normal flow of just being openly human, even in a time of real crisis. He could handle the emergency of a fire, but family things just froze him up.

A couple of days later, Bert was alone at his marina, the place that was kind of his clearing by the lake in the evenings. It was chilly and few boats were on the lake this late in the day and in this kind of weather. The whole world was feeling cold to him. The idea of Jess dying was a bigger pill than he could swallow without a lot of frantic choking. He felt so alone! Then Maggie Welch stopped by, coming by car, not in her boat as usual. She had come to talk. Hopefully, Frank Halstead wouldn't just happen by and then rush off to heat up the village rumor mill again. Jessica surely didn't need that.

"Bert, I've heard the news and I'm so sorry! What can I do to help?"

"Thanks for coming, Maggie. I so need to talk to Jess, you know that very well, but I can't find the words. You and Ed scolded me and really pushed me back in the summer, but I've not made any progress on being open with her. And now time's running out!" How sad that Bert could be so honest and upfront with Maggie, but not with his own wife.

"Maggie, Jess and I have loved each other very much, we really have. We had big dreams together when we first moved out here to the lake, but somehow it's gone dry for us. I'm afraid, just like you two told me, that it's mostly my fault! Can I be forgiven? I'm a good husband in some ways—work hard, am faithful, but I haven't been there for her like I should have, and I know it. Right now, for instance, Joan Mason, a teacher Bud has had over in Pricetown, is at the house taking a turn sitting with her. I probably should be there too, but I don't know what to say or do that would help.

"I know, Bert, and what you really should tell her, you know, about that war business, you just can't bring yourself to do."

"Yea, and it's just more comfortable for me to hang out here. Does that make sense?"

"Yes, it does, in a very sad sort of way. And in response to your question, forgiveness is always possible. When my Herb left me, I grieved for a long time—could hardly feel much of anything. But you need to know this, Bert. Life did come back to me, slowly, differently, finally. Maybe it's too late for your wife—but I hope not for you. Reach out to her, Bert, reach out to her while you still can. Try to be a little vulnerable, even when you don't have any of the right words. Try believing in something bigger than your mill job and this marina. They'll be gone too some day—and so will she!"

"Hey, Maggie, you can't imagine what war can do to a man. Nobody knows it, but I used to write lots of letters to Jess from the Pacific—we were young and I could put many very personal words on paper. Then something happened. I must have gotten hardened and made defensive by the war, and of course there is that terrible killing you know about.

Then I went to work to build a life for us here, but somewhere along the line I got lost in my work, and even from myself. I feel like it's all over now. I hate it for Jess and Bud! He's young, bright, really caught in the middle, and I don't seem to be much help to him. And she's dying and lonely and I can't find it in me to stop either one!"

Tears were in Maggie's eyes, and she was sure that she could spot at least one or two in his. She never before had heard him be so open, so revealing of his deep pain. What then came out of his mouth was an actual pleading, rare indeed coming from Bert Kraemer.

"Help me—somebody help me so I can help them!"

Bert's plea was honest, but so late—and he still couldn't share with his own wife his big secret, his most inner self. He was caught, and his son was caught too, almost fatherless, and doing all he knew to just make it while his mother obviously wasn't.

At the very time that Bert and Maggie were sharing his inner pain and frustration at the marina, Bud was at the clearing. Since a chill was in the air, he was wearing a jacket and holding a school book with gloved hands. He was trembling just a little—and it was more than the cold. A poem was read slowly. His friends would have teased him for pondering something so girlish as a poem, but that didn't matter now. Nothing seemed to matter except that Mom was going away—but not the way she had wanted over the years.

The poem was amazing. It had power to shift the reader to new places, and Bud needed to be drawn elsewhere. StarWalker hadn't come to the clearing today, sadly, unexplainably, but maybe he'd sent the poem instead. After a few lines were read with care, Bud found himself wandering along the halls of other times and the banks of waterways that he'd never seen or even read about. He knew of the Mahoning River, of course, once dammed to form Lake Milton. But none of these rivers in the poetic world were the Mahoning.

The introduction set the scene—the lines had been written by the same Langston Hughes who had created that little thing about the "colored" boy and the carousels with no backs. This poem had the title "The Negro Speaks of Rivers." Bud thought of the harsher word his father would have used instead of "negro." No matter. The man in the poem, whatever his color, was quite amazing.

When only eighteen years old and riding on a train crossing the Mississippi River, that was a really big one somewhere out west, this colored teenager in the poem had scribbled some words on a scrap of paper. This black young man imagined having known some other rivers in other times, some of them ancient, all of them memorable.

"How curious," thought Bud, "that plain old rivers have been so important to people for so long. They are just strips of water forming long and wet lines from here to there on a map; but for some reason they have been waterways of human destiny." Right now Bud needed a little destiny for himself.

This imagining by Hughes was pulling Bud along to those other worlds—and away from the pain of the present. He took his gloves off and the words began to tumble over his fingers and bounce around in his heart, trying to soften, warm, instruct, even cuddle him.

> My soul has grown deep like the rivers.
> I bathed in the Euphrates when dawns were young.
> I built my hut near the Congo and it lulled me to sleep.
> I looked upon the Nile and raised pyramids above it.
> I heard the singing of the Mississippi when Abe Lincoln
>   went down to New Orleans, and I've seen its muddy
>   bosom turn all golden in the sunset.
> I've known rivers;
> Ancient dusky rivers.
> My soul has grown deep like the rivers.

Bud sure needed something for himself that would take him deep, somewhere with a new dawn that then would turn golden in the sunset! Bud blurted his pained thought right our loud. Maybe yelling at the trees would help.

"Mom's going away. I don't want it to be into a dark, silent, colorless night of nowhere where dawns are no more!"

The spell of ancient Africa and old Abe and the somber singing of the Mississippi suddenly was interrupted by another presence, a tardy but very welcome one. It was StarWalker. He reached out one arm toward Bud. He had come when needed in the past, and now he revealed that he already knew about Jessica's cancer and had something important to tell and show Bud.

Once StarWalker was seated, legs folded in good Indian style, the telling began. At first his strange story reminded Bud of one of those Bible stories his mother used to read to him. Jesus had been killed and come back to his disciples looking very alive. They weren't sure it was really him, of course, so he had held out his hands for them to see the wounds from the Roman nails used for his crucifixion. When they saw those ugly wounds, they believed him. In kind of the same way, Bud didn't know what that thing was in StarWalker's hand. It looked like the spoke from a big wooden wheel. Then the Indian asked Bud a question that made no sense—what a time for no sense!

"It's from an old stagecoach, Bud, the spoke of a wheel just like you think. Don't you find that encouraging?"

"No, I sure don't get it."

"Well, I'll just have to explain some more. It's really worth your getting. And after I tell you, the good news is that you can keep this thing for your very own."

Chapter Eleven

FLOODS!

"What do you mean, StarWalker? It's a piece of a what?"

"Well, it's not from one of those famous rivers of the Hughes poet you've been reading. Actually, it's from the wheel of an old stagecoach, Bud."

"Really? I've seen them on TV lots of times. The Lone Ranger likes to stop bad men from robbing them."

"Well, this one is from a real stagecoach. Run your fingers along its smooth shaft. It's yours now, but once it belonged to other people and played a key role in allowing this country to go places and grow. Come to think of it, it's like those rivers in the Hughes poem of yours. It's like rivers of wood instead of water. Wood's amazing stuff, you know. It's life and meaning and strength coming right out of the flesh of these trees and lasting over the generations. I have just this one spoke, but there used to be many of them linking a single rim and hub and making possible the transport of people and goods just like those rivers. My people didn't use them, but yours sure did!"

StarWalker gazed upward, thoughtfully, like he was waiting for preg-
nant yesterdays to yield their fresh fruit and refill his huge memory. Then
he looked back at Bud.

"You remember Joanna, don't you? She's the one who escaped the
big fire out east and fled clear out here. She and the rest of that Hutchins
family came partly on horseback but mostly in a stagecoach with big
wheels. This old spoke is a symbol of their journey, and of their survival,
they and the generations that have followed. When Joanna's grandson
Charles was getting older and still running the family store in Fredericksburg, Ohio, that's when it happened."

"That's when what happened, and where is this Fredericksburg place,
and why is any of this important to me now? My mom's dying and history lessons are hardly interesting to me." Starwalker smiled with understanding and caring.

"Bud, this old town's almost in your backyard, and I can see its significance for you. Let me try to help you see it too."

"Good, my old friend, but you need to know something. I'm only interested in one thing right now—my mom. It's really getting bad!"

"I know, I really do, and I'll get to that shortly. Please be patient, my
son. First, I have to tell you a story."

"A story? OK, let's hear it."

StarWalker began by telling Bud that the story started in the far-off
state of Virginia at about the time of the Hutchins' story up in Connecticut. There had been a town called Fredericksburg and a boy named
George. When he was seven, his family moved to a farm across the Rap-
pahannock River from Fredericksburg. George loved the woods and sur-
veying the land. To him, the woods were a "clearing" something like
Morning Glen is to you. What he couldn't know at first was that the
seeds of revolution and war were already planted and he would grow to
be a major player, even the "father" of a new nation you know as the
United States.

"Do the see the comparison with you, Bud? When so young and just
wandering and trying to sort out life, there was no easy way for young
George to know about destiny things. Neither can you know right now,
Bud. Your home life is revolting against itself. Things will never be the
same again. You will have to stand tall for tomorrow, whatever happens,
maybe even become the father of something new and good."

Bud was fascinated by this strange old man and his latest story about
a kid in the woods and a mysterious Fredericksburg town in Virginia.
Was StarWalker really a man, or maybe a ghost, or even God, or just a
real Indian who hadn't figured out how to die, or what? And the curious

things he was saying—they were beginning to make some sense, and he wasn't done.

"There's something more I'd like to tell you, Bud. Once there was another Fredericksburg town, this one in Ohio and not Virginia. It was a key stop on the stagecoach route from Cleveland to Pittsburgh. Whatever might be left of it now exists right under your beloved Lake Milton."

That was a little too much for Bud. The Indian had mentioned before such a sunken town, but not this clearly, and not claiming that it had been real and right down the street! Bud had guessed the George Washington thing in the early part of the story, but what now? Surely he wasn't about to be told that Abraham Lincoln planted the very trees that enclosed this clearing, or that Craig Beach used to be a cluster of huts along the Nile River in Egypt! He shot a few questions at the story-teller.

"A whole town sunk under the lake? How did the people breathe or eat? How did it get down there in the first place? Is it really still there? Are they all dead? Are you being serious?"

"Easy questions to answer, my son. There was no lake at the time of the town's founding here in Ohio. There soon were mills, taverns, a stagecoach stop, and lots of boys like you running around and laughing and having to work hard. The Hutchins family came here from Connecticut and lived for many moons, three or four generations as your people would say. Then came that awful day, like is now coming to you. Joanna's grandson, Charles, was already old. News arrived on a stagecoach and was told to the town's people by some man from the government in Youngstown."

"What was this big news?"

"It was really awful, Bud. The man said to the people, 'Get ready, all of you. The town is about to die!'"

"How does a town die, StarWalker? I don't understand. Doctors in Warren don't tell towns that they have incurable cancer like they did my mom. So, exactly what happened?"

"It would be a deliberate flood. Some officials in the nearby city had bought lots of land around here and decided to start building a dam in 1913—the very one you know, blocking the water of the Mahoning River and covering nearly 2,000 acres with five to forty feet of water. That would be a back-up supply for those hot mills to the east in Youngstown where your father works, kind of that city's 'western reserve'! Unfortunately, Fredericksburg was in the way and would have to die by being submerged completely. Charles and the others called it 'disaster'; the Youngstown man called it 'progress'."

"The flood, then, was right here? What happened next? Did the whole city drown?"

"Yes, right here. Sinking beneath the flood, slowly disappearing into a watery chaos, yielding to the clutches of liquid death—that's what soon happened to Fredericksburg. People moved away, did whatever they could. Charles Hutchins moved with his family to a nearby farm, and later his son then settled in Craig Beach when the village developed along the new lake."

"Wow! That's quite a story. So our little village has quite a history. I never knew any of this. And what about this spoke from a stagecoach?"

"Well, Bud, like Charles, those who scattered from their homes took little memories with them—like this wheel spoke. Now comes the real point of my story. Something like what happened to Fredericksburg is going to happen to Youngstown itself in a few years!"

"Really? Another big flood, one big enough for all of Youngstown? My neighbor, Mrs. Halstead, says Jesus is coming back soon, but with fire and not a flood, like when God saved Noah and finished off everybody else."

"No, Bud, I'm not talking about the end of the world, only the end of the world that people around here, like your father, have known. Although your father loves the water when he's fishing, or when making money off others who are, this coming flood will be different, but equally devastating for him, and it will end much of what he loves. It will be a huge flow of cultural poison and change, truly disruptive, mill-ending, job-stealing, life-ruining."

That's how StarWalker tied this tragic history to Bud's current situation. It didn't sound very encouraging for the future, especially that of Bert Kraemer. The old Indian was anxious to be sure that Bud understood the meaning he intended.

"I know that you're hardly a little boy anymore, but the boy inside you is still broken, grieving, caught in so many changes. Your mother's coming death haunts you—and it haunts your dad much more than you know. I need to tell you that the Great Spirit's outstretched arms are long and strong enough to reach even you, and even your father. So I have prayed for you, prayed that peace will rain down from heaven on you like joyful little pieces of the sky, like blessed little keepers of the promise that you will be well. May it rain gracious gifts from the stars that want healing for your hurting, like water for those thirsting in the drought of life's losses. That's my prayer for you, my son."

Bud realized that he now was crying. Should he be ashamed? His dad didn't cry, although his mom was crying most of the time, at least when the medication allowed her to be awake enough. Bud would have tried to hide his emotion if his dad were around since it would seem like weakness to him, and his dad didn't seem to respect even a hint of weakness.

But there apparently was no need to hesitate around StarWalker, or the Great Spirit either. They seemed to allow, even honor tears.

Bud now had more than one male role model. He said to StarWalker, "It's really hard to know how being a man and being in tears should to be related." The boy trusted and admired StarWalker or he wouldn't have risked such a comment. So, if he accepted tears and prayed openly to the Great Spirit when in pain, then salty drops running down cheeks must be good, or at least an acceptable thing.

StarWalker looked into Bud's eyes with love and not judgment. Then he said, "Now I need to tell you one more story, Bud, a final one, one I once heard while walking among the stars. It's another echo from yesterday, an important message for your today—and maybe for your dad's too."

"I'm sure listening, my good friend!"

"The mother of a man named C. S. Lewis died when he was only nine years old. This was in England some years ago. She had been her boy's stability and comfort in life. She had been his solid ground, his rock, his park and lake and secret place all rolled into one. Like that city of Atlantis you once heard about at school, she suddenly sank away from all but memory and this Lewis boy was left to swim the dangerous waters of this life almost alone, or so it seemed anyway. His world had been reduced to only sea and scattered islands—the great continent was gone, the lights of the great city were no longer visible, its streets empty, its glory extinguished."

"Sounds like a really big Fredericksburg disaster."

"Yes, and it's kind of a picture of how you'll feel as future things happen to you, my hurting son. Your mom, your continent, is sinking away. And, although you still have your father, he's been lost at sea ever since he came home from the war years ago. You'll understand about that someday, I promise you."

Bud sure understood the business about his mom's sinking and leaving him lost in a storm with no anchor. The business about his dad being lost after the war, however, didn't make any sense, and StarWalker knew it and spoke up again.

"Again, I promise you, you will understand someday. You need to know something else, Bud. You need to know that faith can still be found, a future can still be had for you. That Lewis boy eventually became a great thinker and writer, known and admired worldwide. It may be too late for your mom, in this world at least. You'll have to face that hard fact. She will have no future in this or any other village. Her tent's coming down for good."

"But what about me?"

"You can be well, especially if you do the good thing. Comfort your mom while you still can. Don't run from her pain—and be patient with your dad when he does run." He paused, being sure to choose his words carefully. A young man's life was on the line; it was no time for mistakes with a thoughtless comment, well meaning or not.

"Listen, Bud, don't be afraid to go on toward your own destiny. Your mother would want it that way! And when you leave the village, and you will leave, and regardless of where it is you go, take this wooden spoke with you. Always remember that whole cities have died before and life has gone on!"

That was it. Bud had closed his eyes to let these weighty words find a home inside him. When he opened them again, StarWalker had vanished. No matter. There was no time for thinking any more big thoughts. Bud suddenly realized that it had gotten much darker even though it wasn't that late in the day. Then came the first clap of thunder— unexpected and startling. The storm had replaced the old Indian and was ready to let loose its fury. Bud knew that he had to get home quickly, to the house on Beach Lane that wouldn't be his home forever.

Funny things can run through a boy's mind after an amazing time with StarWalker. But a few drops in the face during the brief bike ride up Beach Lane washed fairly clean his cluttered mind—at least for now. He parked his bike in its usual place and hurried inside. Jessica was awake, maybe because of the thunder. A lady Bud didn't know was sitting with her, and his mother, terribly sick or not, was really worried and had been waiting for him. As soon as he came through the door, she spoke weakly.

"Oh, Bud, I'm so glad you're home! You know your dad says that being near big trees during a lightening storm is very dangerous. I'm sorry, Honey, that it came up so quickly, but obviously you did the right thing, hurrying home to me. It's just that I can't do much anymore but think…and worry...and pray…and wish, wish, wish."

"Wish for what, Mom?"

Jessica's glazed eyes strayed around the room, now a rather plain place not being well kept. "For lots of things, just for things to be different, especially for you, and for your dad too. I don't understand him much of the time. I just wish it were different." She paused, coughed, and then continued slowly and with difficulty, now looking blankly out a window at the driving rain.

"Listen, Bud, I shouldn't have said that. Your dad loves us, I know he does, but you know that something is wrong. I wish I knew what, or who, or whatever. It's been like this since he came back from the war, but it's gotten worse in recent years. I wish I had answers before I'm gone, and I wish you had them too. I'm afraid your dad doesn't have any either."

The "before I'm gone" part of her statement started Bud crying. Jessica was already sorry about talking to her son about Bert in what probably sounded like an unkind way. She felt badly and soon drifted off to sleep—the lady said she had taken her pill just before Bud got home. Having been that open and vulnerable with Bud was unusual for Jessica. She would wake up later and worry again that she had spoken out of turn, violated her private relationship with Bert, and probably added new suffering to young Bud's life. But it was too late to take it back now. She'd have to live with it, although likely not for long, and so would Bud, likely for a very long time.

Within a few minutes the storm had passed. The lady handed Bud three quarters and said his mom had wanted him to ride over to the barber's house and get his monthly trimming. He was glad for the chance to get back outside in the fresh air—seeing his mom like that hurt so much! His bike was quick, those two wheels and all their metal spokes worked flawlessly in unison. That wooden spoke from the old stagecoach was sticking out both sides of the basket attached to the handlebars, like a baseball bat on its way to a non-existent game. He'd better put it somewhere safe when he got back home. StarWalker had told him to keep it always.

"Hello, Mr. Hutchins. Mom said it was my haircut time."

"Sure, sure, come on in, Bud." The barbershop was really only a room of the Hutchins' house three streets over from Beach Lane. Shirley Hutchins was Bud's friend at school. They were quite different from each other, but got along just fine. She was funny, liked being on stage to sing or act in the little concerts and plays at school and even insisted that she'd study someday to be a professional clown. Bud wasn't sure there was such a thing, but if there was, Shirley would be a good one. When he felt way down and hurting inside, he could count on Shirley to make him smile. No school friend was better for him than Shirley, unless it was Delores or especially Betsy.

He'd never met Shirley's mom—people said she was a little odd and rarely left the house. However that was, and people often started rumors that weren't quite right, Shirley was really nice, and Mr. Hutchins was kind and really good with the scissors. And, if they were playing baseball when it was haircut time, he'd always have the Cleveland Indians on his radio, nice and loud for his customers, and maybe even for the neighbors. His ears weren't the best anymore, but his heart and hands were excellent.

The barber always talked as he did his cutting. After some small talk, today something more serious finally came out. "I'm so sorry about your mom, Bud. Wish we could do something to help. Your dad was here last week for his cut—not as much hair as you have anymore!—and he talked and talked about his beloved Jessica. He hurts so much over this thing." Bud knew that this little shop was a great place to pick up village information. It was the alternate bingo place for the non-Catholics. His personal response to the report of Mr. Hutchins about his dad was kept strictly to himself—and it was surprising.

"Then," Bud wondered, "why doesn't Dad show it more at home, all this love he has? Why does he still go down to his marina most evenings when he could be at home. I know he can't really do anything for Mom, but at least he could be there and talk to her gently, telling her what he was really feeling inside. Maybe he just longs for the comfort of the fresh air just as I did in coming over here. Does Dad know that Mom cries and worries so much? Does he cry too, and just not let us know? I've never seen him cry about anything. Maybe he's as scared as me. I wish he'd talk to me about it. He doesn't talk much about really big things." Well, Bert just did talk to Mr. Hutchins. Why at a barbershop and nowhere else? Maybe it was the special setting and chair—when someone gets comfortable enough and made to feel safe, the mouth tends to loosen.

Bud had never talked to Shirley about her family—apparently they had their problems too. But something happened while he was sitting in the barber's chair that made him think maybe he should. And something else happened before his head was made all handsome again. Since there was nothing else to do except hold still, he had found himself looking at some things hanging on the wall across from his chair. One was a tree that had names on its branches. Under the tree's base were the words, "Hutchins' Family Tree." On one branch he could make out the name "Joanna." Next to this curious tree was another frame with the picture of an old stagecoach and the words, "From Connecticut to Ohio, Protected by God."

Bud's mind began spinning like a top, but he managed to keep his thoughts to himself. Could it be? The story of StarWalker was replaying in his mind. He wondered, "Was this Charles Hutchins of Craig Beach related to those people who fled from the British out east? Would his barber know if the Fredericksburg story was true? Maybe Charles had the rest of the spokes from the very wheel his had come from." Bud remembered once seeing the picture of the statue of an old Indian standing in front of a barbershop. Is that where StarWalker had come from, just a picture in his head?

The young man's thoughts were running wild. Maybe StarWalker and Charles were secret friends and that's how the Indian had gotten the spoke in the first place, and how he knew about the old Connecticut business. Maybe when Charles was a baby his mother had run with him in her arms to escape the wall of water coming from the new dam and about to cover everything!" Thoughts kept tumbling over each other.

"Yes, just think of it, my own barber, a survivor of disaster and now only a cutter of hair. Wow! Maybe Mr. Hutchins was two-hundred years old and never aged a day—just like StarWalker! Dare I ask? No, of course not. Dare I tell him what I know? Maybe."

His chance to learn anything was about gone. "All done, Bud. You're looking handsome again. I'll take those quarters and you take your bike on home to your mom. Please give her my best. I know things are bad. I'm so sorry. Greet your dad for me. He's quite a man."

Bud climbed out of the chair, so wanting to ask big questions, and yet he was timid enough to leave his opportunity pass by. He could be wrong and they would sound so stupid, so boyish for a young man. Instead of risking it, he headed straight home, making sure his spoke was safe in the basket. Shirley hadn't been around when he left, but he wondered if she knew about Fredericksburg, or how old her dad really was. Dare he bring it up the next time they were on the school bus? No, 'cause she'd only laugh, putting on her clown face. And worse, if Mike heard such a stupid question, Bud would be sorry indeed. So maybe he'd just keep all this in his imagination. Things were usually safer there anyway.

"Just think of it, though. A family had come all the way from Milton, Connecticut, just to cut my hair at Lake Milton in Ohio!" And there were questions, lots of them. Once in his backyard and sitting in a favorite spot with Lucky jumping in his lap, Bud was free to ask them of himself. "Who knew where StarWalker came from? When's my mom going to die? When she does, will there be new life for her somewhere beyond? Could I visit her there? When she dies and finds out what's next, what will Dad and I be doing? Will we still love her? Will she know that we do?"

The fateful day was only weeks away. It happened mid-day on the couch of the little home on Beach Lane. Jessica just closed her eyes and left her family. And, as was usual, her family wasn't there at the time. Bud was at school and Bert at work. The neighbor lady who was staying with her for that day didn't know it had happened until an hour later. Jessica had felt abandoned in life, and now she had been left by herself in death.

Yes, she was gone, gone far off to somewhere, free at last, free of the questions, the doubts, the high walls of the little village that couldn't be seen but were there anyway. Her secret box in the bank had never been revealed or touched by her for years. Bert knew nothing of it and just kept working and, as before, stayed closed up inside, except for occasional visits from Ed Sinclair and Maggie Welch or a haircut from Charles Hutchins.

As time went on, everybody in the village knew that Bert Kraemer was lonely, even a bit pathetic, but he didn't make it easy for anyone to help. He did have a housekeeper come in once a week, and another lady met Bud coming home from school in the afternoons. She sometimes also cooked the evening meal before Bert could get home from the mill, dirty, tired, and so alone. It was a sparse but workable existence with Jessica gone, but it was temporary, at least for Bud.

Teachers encouraged this bright young man. He worked hard, often hiding in his books as a way of handling grief. Mike even backed off a little. Bud deserved a little space, different as he was. When he finally graduated from the high school in North Jackson, right across the street from Dr. Norton's office, and with honors, he got a scholarship opportunity for college. As his mother would have said, "It's your own ticket out of this village, Honey!"

What should he do with his ticket? It would be hard to leave dear friends like Betsy who seemed content to remain local. Mrs. Halstead, the forever neighbor with endless opinions, let it be known to him that she was worried he might go to a campus with no bingo nights, boredom beyond bearing, and with piles of books added on to the burden. Actually, that didn't sound all that bad to him! Joan Mason counseled him to go without hesitating—and with no concern for lack of bingo or an excess of books. In his heart, she would always be his teacher. He decided to listen to her wisdom, partly because it seemed in line with what Star-Walker had once told him—that he would leave the village eventually and then there would be a new day. He was not to be afraid, but just go.

The goodbye day finally came, a little like the character George in the *Winesburg, Ohio*, novel. It was a sad departure, and yet one probably long overdue. Bud and his dad were together at the house just before he left. Words were needed, but hard to come by. Bert spoke first.

"You sure, son, that you know what you're doing? That college in Pennsylvania is a long way off. I could get you a job in the mill and you could stay here as long as you want."

"Yeah, Dad, I think I do know what I'm doing, and I don't want to stay here. I hate to leave you here all alone, but it's time for me to move on. The mill isn't for me, and I'm not sure it's ever been the best for you either." He paused, swallowing a little awkwardly, and then said to his dad, gently but firmly, what was really on his mind.

"Let me ask you a question, Dad. Do you know what you're doing by staying here alone and just working all the time?" Bert felt the sting of such an important question, but, as usual, he didn't let it show.

"I do, I suppose, as much as anybody ever does. I'm not sure it's the best way, my staying here, but it's all I know and I'll stay with it. And here's what I'd like to know from you. Will you ever come back to the village, Bud?" There was veiled anxiety in Bert's voice, and Bud didn't know the answer to the question. It probably was yes, but only probably. Once out of the village and far away on a campus with new people and fresh learning and different ways, who knew?

They embraced, a welcome new thing for the young man to feel, and a feeling Bert had longed for with Jessica, but now would never have. So Bud left Craig Beach. He took with him two suitcases and that spoke from the stagecoach wheel that he treasured. Going along too, of course, were the little scar on his neck and the red splotch on the back of one hand. And there was one other thing, one very important other thing that he wouldn't even look at carefully for years. It was a treasure chest of his mom's that he managed to fit into one of the suitcases without his dad knowing. Taking it without asking was likely not right, but he had to have something of his mom's. The failure to look into it closely for a long time would be a mistake.

To avoid his dad having to take off work, a friend was going to Warren and would take Bud and his few belongings. There he could catch a train for Pittsburgh and then on east to the college. And, yes, it might be for   good.

Chapter Twelve

WINTERTIME

Bert tried to learn to live alone—there was no choice. He hated it, hated how he had treated Jessica, and struggled with Bud being gone and basically estranged from him. He couldn't get used to the emptiness in his heart and the dryness in his throat—is there no cool and refreshing drink left in this world for a fearful and guilty man? Maggie Welch said there was forgiveness. Then where was it for him?

"I wish that photo had never been taken!" Bert was rummaging through a box of old family photos and there it was. Bud was so cute in that little Navy suit with the white sea cap and all, standing next to his admiring father fully dressed in his uniform from the war. There they were, two proud warriors, son following in his father's footsteps.

"Why did I let them take that? Now it only reminds me that she's gone, he's gone, and he might be tempted to actually follow me and also become a killer!" Bert's hands tightened like he was going to rip it up, but he didn't, burying it instead in the photo pile. It brought back a memory he wanted to stay far away from. Bert didn't blame the Navy so much as himself for what had happened back then. Blame, secrecy, and private shame had been the burden of his life.

Bert was tortured with "what if" regrets. "Maybe I could have grabbed that Jap and held him down until help came. Maybe I could have cornered him on deck, threatened him, and waited for him to surrender peacefully. But no, I was on top of him before I knew it and my training kicked in and he was dead, bloody dead, right in my hands! That foul Oriental never knew it, of course, but he managed to kill me too. I've barely been really alive for thirty years!"

Bert still was living alone in the same little house on Beach Lane fifteen years after Bud had left for school. Most people wouldn't have called it really living. Lack of family, little self respect, shame that would not go away, and fresh fear about a son's future teamed up to slowly tear this man's heart out, chunk by bloody chunk. Not that Bert hadn't tried to repair a few things over time, but repenting to the dead was somehow unable to bring full satisfaction.

It happened more than once, but most dramatically the first time about a month after Bud had first gone off to school. Bert went out to Jessica's grave, sat on a nearby open space near her marker, and just poured out his heart to her—finally coming clean, speaking to her without reserve now that her ears heard nothing and his report could not lead to her rejecting him.

"Why, why didn't I do this before, my love, years ago when you could hear me and hold me and help me and forgive me? I need to tell my story! You deserve to hear it, finally." He was really trying to let out what had festered in him for so long and been so destructive for his family. Is late better than never? Was this a scene of beautiful reconciliation or pathetic remorse? To Bert, unfortunately, it felt mostly like the the latter.

"I'm so sorry, dear Jessica! I'm so, so sorry! I was scared, really scared, and you'll have to understand. If I had told you everything, I thought you might freak out and leave me. I was so stupid, but I really was that scared. Imagine me, the big and strong Navy man and mill worker, tackled for life by a phantom fear, snagged on a rusty hook that has never come out." Bert was now on his knees, right on top of Jessica's grave.

"Jess, it would visit me at the mill, haunt me at the marina, stare at me worst of all when I was at home. It would shake its ugly head, tell me I was done, warn me that I'd better hide if I wanted to survive and protect my family from my taste for human blood. I listened, Jess, listened to my constant visitor, that hated memory. I listened, pulled away from you and Bud, ruined us all by trying to save us. Can you ever forgive me?"

This painful scene continued, threatening to destroy a man who appeared mostly destroyed already. Bert had found among Jessica's things a little diary she had kept in the months before her death. His hands had shook as he dared read it. Her candid thoughts had opened his eyes and just multiplied his pain. Now the pain kept pouring out, dampening the place of the dead.

"Jess, I found your diary and read it. I was amazed to read about all your worrying. You worried that our Bud might be in serious trouble because of some strange Indian in the woods he would visit. I should have known about this too, cared for him like you tried to do, checked that thing out to be sure. But I wasn't involved enough to even know, and you weren't able to break through to me so that you could share your concern. I left you to struggle alone, and maybe let him be in danger without my help—and I'm so sorry!"

Bert hadn't put all that together before. Both he and Bud had been visited regularly over the years. He had been haunted by a taunting spirit of fear and blame and shame; his boy, so he told him before he left for school, had been befriended by a spirit of love and wisdom and encouragement. Bud's friend had called himself StarWalker. Bert's had never given himself a name, but Life-Destroyer would have fit well.

"O, Jess, how wonderful that, in my shameful absence as a father and your struggling as a mother, someone came along to befriend our boy. I don't care whether he was an old Indian, or even a Black guy or a Jap! At least he was there and good to Bud."

Bert's pleading question sat unanswered. "Can you forgive me, dear Jess?" The likely answer, of course, was, "Probably not, not now." How can the dead forgive? But how can the living go on without release from yesterday?

The question was for more than Bert. How can the living choose well the stories out of which they will live and die? How does one pick properly the friends who will model and advise about how life should be lived? Which voices should be heeded? Which images in our heads are the wise ones of conscience, and which only distracting delusions sending us to eventual destruction? Life is about discriminating among the faces, stories, voices, and memories that swirl around, pushing and pulling us in different directions, each wanting to dominate yesterday and direct tomorrow. Surviving life can be hard!

Had Bert not been alone in the cemetery, his pathetic posture on the ground would have been thoroughly embarrassing to him. He had left his knees and slumped down, and then had curled into ball of sobbing flesh.

He'd been destroyed by fear, failed to have faith in the power of his wife's love to overcome an event that so many others had praised.

The questions remained like haunting ghosts out to destroy. Had he acted on that ship as an agent of the devil or of the divine, or neither? Bert had allowed the memory to be twisted into a private horror show that forced him to hide the whole thing from his wife, even as she lay dying. Now everything was gone except the bitterness, sadness, aloneness, and that cold stone with Jessica's name on it. He wanted his on it too so that the pain would end. Maybe in another world she could hear his sorrow and forgive him. Maybe. Maybe she wouldn't want him by her side in death since he hadn't been there most of the time in life!

Bert finally rolled over on his back. He'd been at the cemetery now for nearly two hours and darkness had overtaken the scene. He looked up into the clear night sky. The stars were there, brightly there, but he didn't see them. God was reaching down with forgiveness, but he couldn't feel or accept it. Maybe that strange StarWalker man would come to father as he did to son, but only if welcomed. Bert wasn't open to that kind of thing. Jessica's tears and love were great enough to fill the void of distant space, but Bert's seared soul was not taking it in. What came out of his mouth was only regret weighted down with corrosive memories.

Ed and Maggie had come to see Bert one afternoon at his marina. They knew his problem and urged him to get past it while there still was time, but he shut them up. He ignored their loving words, and continued to keep his real self from his dear wife and son. Now there was just the nagging question. "Was that you, God, you in Ed and Maggie? If so, I'm so sorry I shut them out, and you too!"

The evening was bringing a chill to the air. Bert finally gathered himself up and took himself home, or to what was left of him and home. The weekend was ahead, so no trips to the Youngstown mill were needed. Maybe they'd never be needed again. A letter lying on Bert's table was from the company that owned the mill he'd been working at most recently.

"Laid Off" were the key words in the first sentence. His mill was in financial trouble, as was the whole American steel industry, and it might close forever. Inconceivable until recently, this was a shocking possibility for something so big and so successful for so long! Was another death in the wind? Was it God's judgment? Was it the flood to follow Fredricksburg? Bert was drowning in regret, and big steel was being washed away by foreign competition and its own mistakes.

He didn't leave the house on Saturday, except to hang out at Gerald's Tavern for a couple of hours. Bert wasn't much of a drinker, but a couple of beers went well with finding somebody who wanted to talk about nothing for a while. He ate little all day. Once home again, he read the several letters Bud had sent him over the years since he left. He had kept every one, even though they didn't say all that much, except for bits of news about this or that, a wish that all was well at home, brief courtesy sentiments, etc. But they were something, contact at least, a fragile tie to family.

One thing was clear. Bud didn't hate his father. Bert had wondered why he hadn't written back when Bud had tried to communicate. Bud seemed to be sad, tired of a dead-end yesterday, and only trying to move on with his life. He'd had enough of secrecy, denials, isolation, and refusals to really share. Bert still hadn't helped with any of that, and now they both were paying the price.

Ed Sinclair and Maggie Welch were still across the lake. They had slowed some, of course, but had hardly changed otherwise. Ed had lost Joyce a couple of years earlier and Maggie still lived alone and was managing. They both continued to have good minds and caring hearts, including for Bert when he would let them. Sinclair's store was now owned by a new couple, but Ed continued to stand in the pulpit at the Baptist church every Sunday—he now was saying that his bi-vocational status had changed to uni-vocational. Maggie rarely missed a service, although she wasn't singing anymore—something about her range of notes kind of collapsing.

Bert had been thinking about something for months—other than his own misery, that is. He decided to take a small chance, not big, mind you, but still a chance. After all, it was Sunday morning. He put on some decent clothes—no tie—and showed up at the morning service across the lake (passing on the way the Catholic parish that he had no interest in). No one had any warning of his coming—he'd heard that Baptists liked being warned about things, but he didn't like to do things the way everybody expected. He just showed up and found an empty pew as close to the back as he could.

Winter was coming on. People tended to get isolated more in their homes and question all that was wrong in the frigid world. Ed Sinclair's sermon was on God's faithfulness through the hard times. Bert sat and listened to an old friend.

"When prayers seem unanswered, dear folks, when life itself grows stiff with doubt and the leaves of faith are threatening to tumble to the ground, never forget that God's love never changes!" The pastor went on like that for almost half an hour. Bert noticed that Ed was rather eloquent. Then, without Maggie's help, the little choir finished off the service with all verses of "Amazing Grace." Bert actually knew that song, he guessed from childhood, but he didn't know its reality very much—

he'd never given God's grace much room to work in him. Today he had at least exposed himself to the possibility of learning a little, bending a little, softening a little, being loved a little.

His friends approached him quickly after the final "Amen." "Bert Kraemer, how surprising, how good that you're here!" Both Maggie and Ed joined in the delight while eyebrows were raised on other faces. That's not unusual in a little church when a newcomer arrives, especially one they had heard mixed reports about over the years.

Arrangements were made for something rather foreign to Bert. Ed and Bert were invited to Maggie's for lunch—"eating out" she called it. Bert had never been in her home, even though he knew her well and had known her husband Herb since they served together during the war. Herb, of course, had disappeared years ago to begin another family with a younger woman, and, sadly, Bert hadn't seen him since.

It was a really good meal, not the scraps and leftovers and quickies that Bert fed himself on most other days. Once the meal was over, things gave way to more serious conversation. Bert announced his loss of work. That was added to the coming of winter that would keep his marina basically closed until spring. He admitted to being deeply discouraged.

"Let's face it friends, life's moving on for us all. I'm about done, I think. Life is deserting me like I've deserted it for decades. That seems fair enough, doesn't it?" One could now see pain in Ed's face.

"Bert, I know you didn't come today for any religion to be pushed on you, but you're reaching out nonetheless for a more active friendship, and maybe for a flicker of some kind of hope. Just know that we're your friends and we love you, we really do. Maybe just knowing that will bring a little hope."

"Maybe, and I do thank both of you. You know my big problem over the years, and how poorly I've handled it, and you've loved me anyway. That's kind of amazing, come to think of it, like your song this morning in church—sorry you didn't sing, Maggie, it would have sounded even better if you had."

She smiled, embarrassed and pleased at Bert's surprising compliment.

"It reassures me, helps me finally to believe that Jessica and Bud could have loved me too, even if they'd known, even though I just couldn't tell them. Now you two might as well know something. It's pretty personal, but I'll tell you anyway. I've cried out to Jessica, time and time again, or at least to her memory, pleading for her forgiveness— too late, of course, much too late. Now I need to try somehow with my son. We'll see if that's too late too. I'm not even sure if I have his right address anymore."

Maybe it was a Baptist thing, Bert wasn't sure. Anyway, they ga-thered around him where he was sitting and put their three hands on his shoulders and head. Since Ed was the pastor and had only one hand, he put his on Bert's forehead and pronounced a blessing on him while Mag-gie quietly mumbled amens.

"May God shine his light on you, Bert, in your darkness. May God give you fresh vision in your blindness, our brother, and fill your bleed-ing heart in all its emptiness, and finally somehow release you from fear's terrible grip and give you God's peace! And, in your eternal love and with your amazing grace, pave Bert's way back to his son."

Removing his hand, Ed realized for the first time that Bert was fe-vered and surprisingly frail. Not only dignity had drained away, but maybe health too. Without saying anything, Ed told himself to call Dr. Norton tomorrow. Yes, he was still practicing medicine, but only three days a week now, and with limited hours even on those days. Ed thought the doctor needed to see Bert right away.

Departing time had come for this special Sunday. Maggie embracing Bert tenderly, kissing him on the cheek for the first time in her life. She also noticed with sadness his physical distress. She glanced at Ed. They both knew that something was very wrong.

Chapter Thirteen

A TRUNK AND A TREASURE

I suppose you'd have to say that he'd stolen it. Bud didn't want to think of it that way, of course. It was his mom's and he at least should have asked his dad if he could have it. But Bert had been busy at the time he was packing to leave for college, and Bud had acted on impulse, not wanting to risk a negative response if he had asked.

Jessica's death had been so hard for the young man. He had wanted to take with him something very personal of his mom's—likely all he'd ever have again. He had chosen the little chest filled, he presumed, with personal stuff of his mom's, and maybe his dad's too, little things like pieces of cheap jewelry, stray coins, a few favorite receipts, just trinkets of yesterday, whatever she'd stuck in there. He'd seen her occasionally handle it lovingly, even appear to hide it when she was done. He didn't think that his dad was particularly sentimental and might not miss this little chest. Maybe he'd never even noticed she had it.

It was easy over the years to ignore this chest. When he thought about, and that was rarely after a while, he always had a good feeling just knowing that he had something of his mom's, tiny and meaningless as he presumed it was. He always kept it safe, thoughtlessly regarding it as a reassuring but unexamined piece of nostalgia. By doing this, he told himself, he was defying the ravages of time like his mom's body had failed to do. The chest, even if worthless to anyone else, never changed and kept him within reach of his mother.

Bud had quickly become absorbed in college studies and social activities. No one on campus knew him as the son of a reclusive dad or a crying mother. People didn't know that he came from a culturally vacant village or once was thought to be on the edge of insanity because he saw and talked to an old Indian who maybe wasn't there. He was an excellent student, an avid reader very curious about the wider world. He dated a little, but never seriously. In fact, given the past, Bud doubted that he would ever want to marry. Memories of his mom and dad had soured that idea for him. Even so, he occasionally thought about Delores and Shirley, and especially Betsy back home. They had been special, but that was a long time ago.

He couldn't help but wonder sometimes. Had Delores ever actually seen the dragon? Did Shirley ever become a real clown? Had Betsy ever married—the lucky guy, whoever he was. And he often thought about his dad, even sending a letter to him once in a while, although finally deciding to leave it at that. He never heard back and finally quit sending anything.

Time flew by quickly. One day college was behind Bud. Another graduation with honors and Mr. Bud Kraemer's own teaching career had begun. To no one's surprise, his chosen field of specialization was English literature, a natural extension of the good teaching of people like Miss Mason when he was a boy. Good teachers, after all, are to be found in out-of-the-way places like Pricetown, Ohio, and their good efforts linger for a long time. In fact, Bud was almost emotional one day when he assigned some of the poetry of Langston Hughes to his students. Suddenly he recalled his first exposure to this American master of meaningful words.

"Thanks, Miss Mason!" he mumbled to himself. She had done the first introducing, and had made sure that the significance of this poet's work didn't get past Bud.

On another day, it happened suddenly. Out of nowhere, one ring of Bud's phone sounded without warning and changed life itself. The call was from Dr. Norton back home. Once Bud realized who he was talking to, he was surprised that old John was still alive, and that he had figured out how to find him, and that there was any agenda between them to discuss. Although basically retired from his medical practice, John Norton was very much alive and quite aware of the ongoing lives of some of his former patients who still lived around Lake Milton. Bert Kraemer was one of them. Jessica had died years before despite what John could do for her, but Bert had now lived a full life, longer if not happier. Finally, however, his mind maybe and his body for sure were weakening badly.

"Is this Bud Kraemer?"

"Yes, who's calling me from Craig Beach? I recognize the phone code and haven't been in contact with anyone there in years."

"It's Dr. Norton, son, someone who's known your parents for a long time. I need to tell you something very important. Your dad is facing his last days, Bud. If you want to see him one last time, you'd better come soon. He's in a nursing home in Pricetown near where you went to school. So far as I know, I'm one of the few who's visited him recently, except for Ed Sinclair and Maggie Welch. They're the ones who called his condition to my attention. He's kept to himself mostly since you left for college and just doesn't have friends or family—except you. His old marina is gone now, replaced by a bigger one belonging to someone else, and soon his eyes will be closed too.... Are you hearing all this, son?"

"Yes, I'm hearing, and thanks so very much for the call, doctor. I'll make travel plans right away. I'm glad you're OK, and also thanks for your kindness to my parents over the years. I know my mother confided in you sometimes when she couldn't talk to anyone else, including Dad. Thanks for listening to her and being a little light in her life. She surely needed you at critical times and you were there for her. I'll try to be there for Dad if I can, at least a little."

"You're welcome, son. By the way, one more thing. You surely remember Maggie Welch and the local grocer and Baptist pastor, Ed Sinclair? I saw her at the weekly bingo game just last night—she started coming after your mother died. Ed had already called me, but she's the one who finally convinced me to call you. She used to have good talks with your dad. In fact, she told me that she and Ed talked to him together once or twice about very important things, and now you really need to do the same while you can."

"I'm willing to try, doctor, although I'm not sure what there is of importance that he'd be willing to discuss. He was never good at that kind of thing. Still, given what you say, I'll be there in a couple of days and give it a try."

"And still another thing, Bud. Maggie also said something about letters your dad had written to your mom during the war. I hope you have them. If you do, you should find and read them before you come. Your dad told Maggie some months ago that Jessica's personal treasure chest is missing and he thinks the letters are in there and that you probably have the chest. He hopes so."

"I do have it, Dr. Norton, but I didn't know there were letters in it. I'll read them right away. Thanks for the tip."

"Before I hang up, Bud, I need to tell you something else. While this was never my business, I happen to know that there used to be a little key in that chest—your mom told me that once when she was in my office. If you find it, be sure to take the key to the local bank in North Jackson, the one just down the street from my office, and see if it opens one of their security boxes. Your mom used to have a box there without your dad knowing it, and she told me there was a lot of money in it."

"Letters and a key—and money? This is all news to me. Well, I have the chest and I'll check on what is in there after this call. If I find any letters and a key, I'll do as you and Maggie suggest. And I really do appreciate the call, doctor! Bye."

The treasure chest was pulled out of his closet and opened almost immediately. He hadn't paid any attention to it for years, but now it would feel good to finger the past while preparing to go back for a final visit. Were there letters in there, and a key to money? What his fingers touched gave him a welcome feeling of excitement and expectation. There was a whole stack of letters, a little yellowed and with rubber bands around them. The first one he touched snapped. It was brittle and virtually useless anymore. Would it be the same for the letters— interesting but without meaning after all these years? And a key? Yes, there it was!

Bud fingered the key, wondering if money still would be in a bank box, or if that was just another part of his mom's dream life. The key was in a tiny red folder with the bank name printed on it, and there was a box number there too. He'd check on this when he got a chance, but seeing his dad would come first.

Questions were now inevitable. "Where would my mom have gotten lots of money? Maybe she hadn't, or it now was gone." As for the letters, there must have been two or three dozen of them, all written in longhand, very readable, only slightly faded here and there. Bud settled into his favorite chair and began to handle them gently and read them thoroughly. Forty-five minutes later, hardly having moved a muscle in the meantime, he put the last one down and looked blankly out the window, having just met a man he hadn't known before. In fact, Bud almost wanted to apologize to his dad for violating his privacy. Reading these letters was like looking deep into a man's heart, and sometimes even into his bedroom at night as he was with his wife.

Bert had gone to sea as a young married man. War had been experienced by him as hours of horror separated by days or even weeks of sheer boredom and meaningless activity. Into his second year away, and longing for the war to be over and his going home, he had started the writing—or at least writing the letters that had survived. Nearly all had a "BJ" on them, two letters lovingly linked so closely and surrounded by a heart—he hadn't known that his dad was into symbols and artwork. Obviously, this particular symbol was a secret sign between Bert and Jessica pointing to an intimacy in love never to be broken by war or peace, ocean or river, time or eternity.

Bud's overall response to the letters was pure surprise. "Wow! My dad wrote these?"

The later the date of a given letter the more intense it was with his talk of sexual fanaticizing with his dear Jess, graphically expressed memories of their being together early in their marriage, concern about the world their children would have to grow up in, and dreams of what a weary warrior wanted for BJ and baby B after he got home. Bud had just discovered a sensuous man, an intimate sharer with his dear wife, a dreamer, an intensely devoted family man, an articulate lover who detested war and longed for a soon-coming peace. What a picture of an ideal father, one he'd never met before!

Bud kept staring and wondering. Why over the years had the man in Craig Beach and now languishing in a Pricetown nursing home been so different from the truly sensitive and romantic writer of these letters? What had happened to ruin a truly wonderful man? Maybe his dad would explain things to him—that is, if Bud got the chance to be there in time and his dad was finally willing to share. He had to get on the road—and fast!

Whatever had so injured, derailed, polluted, and almost sunk his dad after the letter-writing days was now a big question for Bud to try to get answered. The problem now beginning to drive the son was his managing to get to the dad in time, telling him that he finally knew what an amazing man he really was—or at least had been, despite whatever curve life had thrown at him. He so wanted to tell his dad that he loved him as never before, and that he wanted so much one day to become like him, the real him, the early him, deep, sensitive, loving.

So much for entertaining these life-changing thoughts where he was in eastern Pennsylvania. Bud had to pack quickly and hit the road.

"I'm coming, Dad. Wait for me!!"

Chapter Fourteen

NIGHT ON THE LAKE

He'd had always hated those pesky mosquitoes! They would swarm around a boat toward evening, especially if any light was present. They were good blood hunters, just trying to survive like Bud was. Tonight was slightly different, though, not at all like his occasional boyhood ventures on the lake with his dad. Bud was careful to spray himself with repellent. He would keep it as dark as possible because he wanted to see the stars, and his mind was so preoccupied that he probably wouldn't notice a few silly little bites anyway.

Bud had been told by the attending nurse in Pricetown that it looked like a meaningful visit with his dad would have to wait until at least the next day. Bert Kramer was heavily medicated and not conscious. So Bud chose to try relaxing a little, driving slowly around the village streets trying to remember and seeing if he just bumped into somebody he might recognize. He hadn't—how odd to be here and feel almost like a stranger! As the day wore on, he found a pay phone and called Pricetown, getting the same delay message confirmed. So he decided that he would visit his mother's grave and then seek the solace of the lake itself. Stuck in his mind was something his mom used to say.

"Well, Honey, in the grand scheme of things...." What an interesting phrase that is. Now that he actually thought about it, he wondered what his mother had meant. "Is there really a 'grand scheme,' or just 'things'? What had his mom thought, or did she just mindlessly say this now and then?" As Bud stood at her grave, he hoped with all he had in him that there was a grand scheme to life and that his mother was now enjoying its fruits—at least if they were good. He, of course, had no idea that once his father had curled on the very ground now at his own feet. Bert had cried like a baby, feeling so guilty and helpless. Bud cried too, but more with gratitude for what good there had been.

And there was something else from childhood that kept coming to Bud's mind. He couldn't help but wonder about SkyWalker. He hadn't seen him for years, but in some ways it seemed like only yesterday. Was he still alive? Had he ever been? Was he always with Bud's subconscious, never to die? There was no one he could ask, of course. Maybe the answer wasn't that important. That old Indian had always come to his mind when he saw or felt or remembered various things from years past.

Less than an hour later, Bud had left the cemetery, returned to the village, and begun walking down to the beach. He had decided to rent a boat for the evening. He was surprised to see a lovely amphitheater sitting there, with the opening of the curved shell pointed westward to catch sunsets before dark fell. He could envision a crowd of locals gathering on the grass and sand on summer evenings to watch some movie or hear a new band try to play in public for the first time—and likely for the last. This was Craig Beach, after all, hardly Nashville or New York! The only scouts around here were the advance guard of the mosquito world looking for the best blood pickings for the evening.

But sarcasm was hardly appropriate. Bud had to admit that, Craig Beach or not, this bandstand was a lovely little place from which to watch the stars high above. It was, Bud thought, the village's modern version of his old Morning Glen. He now longed for some solace from somewhere, including from high up among the twinkling lights, or even from the deep darkness that surrounds each speck of light up there. Then a heavy thought saddened him.

"Actually, in total, there's much more darkness than light in the night sky. Why is life like that too? Dad was once full of light, and then somehow the larger surrounding darkness had closed over him, snuffed him out. How---why? Was there any light left in his crumbling body and shadowed soul?"

Bud intended this as a late evening of deep thinking, about his mom and dad and himself, about the past and the future, about the why of things in general. And it already had begun, even before he could get away from the shore in his floating rental. A little sadness was natural when getting a boat from somebody other than his dad and at the very spot where the old Kraemer marina had been. A little nostalgia for Star-Walker was to be expected too. Bud needed more than hours of random thoughts out on the open water. He needed wisdom. Hopefully, getting that need met was not merely wishful thinking.

With only little bits of the light above, and so much darkness surrounding every star, and with his father out of commission, soon forever, and no StarWalker aboard, Bud was on his own. He pushed off from the dock, moving out into a private nowhere. He had a motor on the back, but wouldn't use it unless necessary. The oars are quiet if handled carefully in and out of the water, and the rhythm of their motions can be almost hypnotic. He preferred the quiet of rowing, the propulsive rhythm of muscle and will and water. He could dig into the lake's yielding surface as deeply as he felt most comfortable from minute to minute. Rather than the old woods, he was trying a water get-away. Lake water, especially when there is barely a breeze, has its special way of shimmering in the dying sunlight and refreshing every new minute—unless, of course, a man got lost in the darkness or run over by a late-night speed boat taking a quick spin before bed!

The surface of a lake can have many personalities. Especially when the day's light fades and the evening breeze ruffles the water, colors darken, air cools, and perceptions of what is real and what is merely imagination get confused. A man alone in a small boat senses isolation setting in—just what Bud wanted. He remembered once visiting caverns in central Indiana. Running for many miles underground is a river, fifty-five degrees all year and with nothing alive except a few blind fish and crabs that were white—no eyes needed and no color sustained in this perpetual darkness and wet silence.

Being down there with solid rock overhead, a paid visitor from the upper world can find each minute frightening, cleansing, disorienting, maybe reorienting. For the blind little fish, innocence and purity are possible because of the bliss of ignorance and a complete disconnect from the world outside. For a hurting man, such bliss may be preferable to life as usual above the thick rock ceiling. The world can seem so innocent when it's lost from sight. But when the light returns, so does the fuller truth, the cold and harsh truth about things as they really are.

For Bud, the privacy on this evening was a privilege. Even above ground, the real world tends to evaporate and another and more real world slowly emerges. Overhead was not a weighty and threatening ceiling of heavy rock, but a vast and endless mystery, a black lid on the world, one that was full of pinholes for countless eyes of eternity to peek through. That's exactly what Bud hoped for himself out on Lake Milton this night. He wanted to fill his eyes and soul with the millions of hints of eternity overhead.

He'd already talked as much as he wanted today, mostly to a teenager running the shiny new marina on the very spot where his dad's had been. Is nothing sacred! He had asked the young man about Frank and Hazel Halstead. The boy said he knew of them, but was pretty sure they were both dead. Maybe Hazel had yelled out her last "bingo!" and Frank had started his last rumor—unless the news of his death was itself only a rumor. The village surely would be a duller place without those colorful people.

And what about Joan Mason? Wouldn't that teenage boy have gone to the same grade school Bud had attended? But, no, he said he hadn't even heard of her. She had been such a good teacher for Bud. Maybe she had read so many book reports on that *Winesburg, Ohio*, novel that she just had to get out herself. He wondered whether she had gone to teach in a bigger Winesburg somewhere, and by now had left there too. That seems to be the way of things. The shine tends to wear off almost anywhere once life just beneath the surface is sampled and then sours. Craig Beach had been great for the Kraemers, and then for some reason it wasn't great at all.

Profound questions come more easily when you're out alone on a lake of mirrors and shadows. Answers aren't readily available, but the imagination is freed. What really swims or lies in the black depths below, and what or who flies free in the now twinkling sky high above? Time and distance were already losing their grip on Bud as the small waves slapped gently on the sides of his boat and rocked him in the bosom of nature. Out there alone, there is only isolation, and certainly nowhere to hide. A man gets covered up in darkness and becomes thoroughly exposed. It is a mysterious escape, a hopeless imprisonment, just what one sometimes really wants and needs.

Bud was in great emotional need. Sometimes he would row hard, like he was trying to get away from something, and sometimes he would just drift aimlessly, letting the tired oars lie randomly in the water. There were no strong currents to worry about and only a few speedboats still sporting around in the distance despite the lateness of the day. He had the mandatory lantern; it came with the boat rental. It could be seen by any other boater who might stray dangerously in his direction. However, unless one of them did come close, he didn't want to be seen and shut it off.

Shining the lantern seemed like an abrupt intrusion on the mystery of the night, and it attracted those annoying mosquitoes.

Basic fishing equipment had come with the boat, so Bud finally put a line in the water, even though his mind was lost somewhere in the sky and his heart broken for his dad. Bud's eyes had long since left the pole that he had left resting carefully on the side of the boat. Suddenly, the pole lurched, almost falling over the side! Bud grabbed it and realized that something large and heavy was down there and on his line. However, as he frantically reeled it in, it didn't jerk back and forth like the usual struggling fish. It hung heavy and came willingly, the way he hoped to approach his own future. He had plumbed the depths mindlessly and yet had gotten lucky—or so he thought.

When his big catch finally broke the surface, barely visible in the moonlight, it was a big surprise. It was a large boot! Had he found...could it really be?...another leftover of old Fredericksburg down there? A man's leg hadn't survived, but had his boot? Once in his hands, however, Bud knew that it was not nearly that old. In fact, it had stamped on it the initials of the mill where his dad used to work. Too bad. Not much left of Fredericksburg or the mill anymore. He tossed the thing back over the side to rejoin the sacred remains that might be down there somewhere.

He kept thinking about that nursing home. If he did get to talk to his dad the next day, he wouldn't say a word about this big catch. He'd get teased without mercy, that is, if his dad had the energy. Even so, Bud thought about how strange it is that a man could get lost in that upper vastness of the night sky and then suddenly get pulled back to a more mundane reality by a little jerk on the line from a boot that had been lost somewhere below.

Were the remains of old Fredericksburg really down there? More importantly, was there a God way up there? Does God send down to his creatures hints of his will with a hook that he hopes will bring them up to him? Well, at least there still might be a hungry fish below that would be willing to grab for some food and unintentionally gain the attention of a lonely man. It didn't really matter. This man was busy reaching upward with his very soul, reaching toward some divine bosom on high that could comfort and guide. There was a hook—the fish's potential demise; there also was a spiritual void, one man's attempt at faith, a soul wanting to be hooked by something eternal. Bud could talk to himself freely out here. His musings tended to be questions.

"What if there is only an endless nothingness up there, or a black and wet nothingness down there? What if there is no "grand scheme," only a mass of "things" that just bump into each other accidentally and then are gone forever? On the other hand, there could be an amazing grace reaching my way to bring a humble man upward to the skies, clean and new and alive forever. I sure hope and pray that there is!"

The moonlight above and the mundane below. What a crazy combination we always seem caught up in. We are drawn by the one in our pain and deadened by the other, brightened by a false hope and finally washed away by the endless emptiness of life, unless we are saved finally by a divine grace we don't deserve. On the other hand, there is so much apparent evidence that we go in circles like that old park merry-go-round, sometimes enjoying the ride for a time, but always getting nowhere.

"No!" Bud blurted aloud, scattering dozens of mosquitoes in the process. "I'm not going to live all of my life in a cesspool of fatalism. Maybe there's no explanation for Mom's early death, and now my poor dad struggling so hard, but life is a choice. Yes it is! Faith, even without final answers, is a viable option—one I so much want to choose!"

Bud's family had been saddled by quiet cynicism and constant denial for as long as he could remember. He looked up into the vast night sky and announced to whoever was out there that he was done with it! He was tired of wallowing in cynicism; he was ready to believe.

Bud was a mature adult now and no longer needed his father's permission to roam off with the boat, staying all night if he wanted. His mom would have been so fearful for her boy, likely lost in the darkness of the night like she felt she was all the time, even in the daylight. But he knew the lake well and had brought a blanket, coffee, and a sandwich. They had been bought at the new store that used to be Sinclairs. Maybe he would stay out until daylight would expose him again to the eyes of others. He needed to think, maybe pray, and definitely be alone—unless there really is a God, in which case Bud didn't want to be alone ever again!

This night on the lake offered a chance for Bud to get a grip on himself, maybe a handle on the future, maybe a mindset to go back to his dad with his heart right. He had some apologizing to do! Out here on the water, with everything supporting you and nothing judging you, it was easier to ask life's big questions, and more likely that some answers would be found.

"What about the God thing? Is God the One who not only walks among the stars, but put them there in the first place? Does God sometimes speak to people through prophets, special voices who walk among the stars and come to the clearings of our lives with special wisdom from yesterday, wisdom that might guide tomorrow? Does God hurt when we hurt, carry the scars of our worldly crises? Once having been touched by God, and having met one of his prophets in some private clearing, are we to become divine agents to others, little StarWalkers ourselves? Can Mom see me out here, and does she still love me, and is all of her hurting really over?"

Slipping into and out of one bay after another, Bud had been free all night to smile and cry and think as much as he wanted.

"Oh, to be a boy again, but not the anxious boy I was. I want to be a real 'Bud,' a fresh flower from God's hand that can bring some beauty to others—especially to my father." Bud now wanted to focus on simple things, with his days not defined by computer crashes, paperwork, surviving months with more days than cash, constant gossip and empty small talk, credit card bills, terrorist attacks, and all the rest. He had found the big city another village, just on a bigger scale. People without vision and faith get trapped wherever they are. What about the power of a smile, dreams—even of imagined fiery dragons or ancient Indians? What about making angels in the snow, finding beauty in a secret clearing, having faith that can overcome the world?"

Bud had realized that the best travel might not require a plane ticket or passport. It might not involve escaping the perceived imprisonment of life's confining circumstances. One can encounter wonder close at hand—or at least it used to be possible. Bud determined that it would be again! Tomorrow would be another trip to the nursing home. It might be the last, wrapped in total sadness, or maybe it would be the first when he could actually talk to his dad and share the new insights and even some joy rooted in faith and not fear. Bud surely needed that talk to happen. So did Bert, whether or not he realized it. There was so much that needed to be said. But would the opportunity be there?

Chapter Fifteen

YOU WROTE THESE?

Bud stepped into his dad's room one more time. It was small and so cramped after the wide openness of the lake. Bert's world had truly closed in on him, leaving him almost no room to move anymore! He was asleep like before, but the nurse said he should be awake shortly. So Bud pulled a chair closer to the bed, sat down, and found himself looking closely at his father's face. It was hardened with work and age, and yet strangely gentle and peaceful.

It took a strong mind and body, and a lot of pride and daring, to do what he had done. His was the generation that had defeated tyranny on a worldwide scale. They then had come home—those who made it—to transform piles of red dirt and scrap into molten metal that was poured, blasted, pounded, and rolled into various shapes of steel used to support the mainframes of modern civilization. The Homestead Works was just one of the massive plants in the Youngstown area, and this dying man had worked in several of them. In Bert's time, and in that of his father before him, that Homestead place had rolled out steel for the Panama Canal, the Empire State building, the United Nations building, the San Francisco Bay bridge, and much more. Wow!

A nurse stepped into the room to check some reading on one of the machines. What a contrast—a man helping to build a bigger and better world and now the same man able to do no more than register numbers on a little screen. She left the room, allowing Bud to resume his reflections.

Bud's heart reached out for a better understanding of this simple and yet amazing man lying there, more helpless than the little boy he remembered being. What gives life meaning, after all? Bert, at least for much of his life, seemed to think that it's vigorous effort, hard physical work, using the muscles of the body to make things happen, to move things, control things, create things. At least, that's how Bud had known him. Sweat dribbling down the body—that's real, that makes you know you're alive and worth something. Now, however, Bud feared that what his dad thought significant was done, gone. No more sweating; no more worth.

"No!" Bud's heart cried out. "Dad, wake up and let me tell you that the answer is no!"

When those mills shut down, the money had gone away, many things slowed to a crawl in the area, and finally even Bert's marina had been forced to close. A strong and independent man had been reduced to thinking that he wasn't anybody worth loving. Then came the fancy new marina on the same little bay—workable in a poor economy because it was built and subsidized by some rich guys in Youngstown. —a little like Jessica who had thought that she never had been anybody especially important.

The nurse walked into the room. "Is he OK?" asked Bud. "I've noticed some movement. Does that mean he's waking up?"

"Yes, a little. It's time for his shot. Step out for a minute, please. This might finish waking him up for you and you can come right back in."

It did. Bud was invited back into the room and Bert recognized him immediately. Words of gratitude and commitment started to tumble out of Bud's mouth. He so wanted to understand and show proper respect while the chance remained. He was here for this very reason, and he also had some important things to ask.

"Dad, I'm here, and I'm so glad you're awake, and so glad to be home with you!"

Bert spoke slowly, and with a little slur, but quite understandably. "Hi, son, I knew you'd be here." He hesitated, reaching for more strength to keep talking. "Love can beat the negative thinking, son, stuff that's had me trapped for years, and kept us apart."

"Yes, love, it's real! And, Dad, I apologize for taking Mom's little treasure chest when I left years ago. I wanted something to take with me and I should have asked."

"It's OK, boy. I looked for it a couple of times, wasn't sure what she had in it, and then put it out of my mind. No harm done. Wish I'd kept one of my own, but never took the time."

"Dad, thanks for understanding, but you need to know that her chest had some amazing stuff in it. There were letters, dozens of them from you to her during the war. I've read them just recently, over and over. My eyes have been glued to many of the words. Maybe they weren't my business, and in one way I'm sorry for reading them, but I couldn't help it."

Bert let some seconds pass before he responded. He squirmed in the bed, looking for that more comfortable position. "You've read my old letters? I didn't know that she'd even kept them, and I hardly remember what they say. That was a long time ago when things were very different, Bud. I'm not so sure I'm happy with you having done that. It's like peeking into our bedroom!"

"I know, Dad, and I'm truly sorry, but I couldn't help it, and doing it has made me think differently about you—and in a really, really good way."

"Hey, things and people change. Keep whatever I said back there to yourself. Even though hard, those were the good days!"

"I understand that, Dad, and I'll keep the letters to myself, you can be sure of it, but here's what I want to say now. Please listen carefully."

"I'll try. If you see me doze off, jut wait or punch me or something." They both grinned and Bud continued.

"There are some beautiful thoughts in those letters, Dad, ones straight from your heart like I never heard from you before. I'm convinced that deep somewhere in you those same values and emotions and commitments still exist. You really did love Mom! You missed her terribly when you were far away and scared, and you also had the words to tell her in ways she could really hear."

Bert's eyes had gotten noticeably bigger. "I sure was scared and lonely back then! I wish that later on things could have worked better than they did."

"Your words may have failed you later, Dad, but not back then! And that's not all. You said things, truly wonderful things *about me*. You need to know that I've cried and laughed now that I know how much you really loved me. Why didn't you ever tell me that when I was a hurting little boy? I so needed to hear that from you! Understand, I'm not angry, just sad and wondering why."

Bert was stunned. Bud was giving him no way of running from his own emotions, his own brokenness, his own failed past, and the much more that actually was inside him—somewhere—that had been trapped and stunted for so many years. Bert shouldn't run, of course, he should never have run away from his feelings, but he'd done it for so long that he wasn't sure how else to be anymore. Bud was wanting to shower love on his dad, and do it by reminding him of his better self. He heard Bud saying heartfelt things, and it felt so good!

"Dad, I love you. Do you hear me, I love you! Whatever was wrong before, let's make it right now!"

"I hear you, boy, I hear you loud and clear, but I'm not sure I'm worth it. I didn't help your mom like maybe I could have, and I wasn't a good father to you, and I don't deserve forgiveness and love. I worked hard, always, and tried to provide and be faithful. Sadly, that's about all I did. There should have been more, I know. I'm going on now to let the Big Judge deal with me."

"Dad, I've got other things to tell you before you go anywhere. I've never been a church person, you and Mom didn't show me how, but that's no matter anymore, and I'm not here to judge you for that either. Once, long ago, Hazel across the street from our house—do you remember her?--told me from the Bible about the Spirit of God. I already knew about the Great Spirit from another friend, an old Indian, but that's a long story I won't get into. Here's what I want you to know. I've met this divine Spirit now, very personally, met him on the lake last night, and I've asked for forgiveness for you and me and Mom, and I got it! I'm free, and you're free, and she's been free for years. And you're right, Dad. You don't deserve it, and I don't either. But that doesn't matter! Love is bigger than our deserving!"

Bert and Bud fell into silence, looking in wonderment at each other. Forgiveness.... Love.... Reconciliation? The air smelled of medicine and disinfectant, and yet the same air was pleasantly pure and wholesome. Neither of these men had breathed deeply and healthfully like this in their lives. Even though the room was small and crowded with equipment, it now seemed like open space without boundaries. Finally, Bert broke the spell.

"I love you Bud, I love you so much! Thank you for coming to see me and telling me all this!" Bert choked, first out of joy and then because he couldn't breath. Bud helped him and the nurse came rushing in. The problem passed, at least this time. Apart from the choking, this was a magically wonderful time, marked by grace from above and joy within.

"Dad, now that you're OK again, there's something else. In my mother's little chest was more than the letters. Are you feeling well enough for me to tell you about this too?"

"Yeah, I think so. Go for it. I didn't know anything about the stuff in that chest, so surprise me again if you think I can stand it."

"Here goes, Dad. There was a key in a folder with a bank name on it. I went yesterday after roaming around the village. I told the bank people who I was. They knew that Mom had died and let me use the key. In the security box I found $10,000 in cash! With that huge pile of money was a note to you, Dad, now to us I guess. It says that the money was her dad's. She got it when he died, and you never knew. She kept it as her "dream dollars," her way out. Do you see? There's good news here. Mom always had money to escape the life she felt trapped in, and she never used it. It had to be because she couldn't bring herself to leave you, Dad. Her love for you bigger than her pain! The only question now is, what do we do with it? What are our dreams?"

"Wow! That's somethin'. Maybe she did continue to love me even when I made it hard for her. She had her ticket to anywhere, you say, and she didn't use it, and that's 'cause of me? What a wonderful thought!"

Bert was crying—more cleansing, more connecting with Bud, and especially now reconnecting with his Jess, long gone and yet back with him in a fresh way. He thought and thought about Bud's question, maybe even prayed about it when his eyes were shut. He actually fell asleep, newly relaxed with life enough to risk voluntarily closing his eyes—even if they never opened again. If they didn't, no matter. He now knew he'd be fine, very fine in some better place, and maybe not alone there anymore. There'd be the Big Judge, but he'd have a Jesus smile on his face. And there'd be Jess, arms outstretched, thrilled that finally her Bert had come home to her—and to stay this time.

Bud waited patiently for an answer. What about the money? It was still his dad's call. Bert's eyes eventually came back open. A little groggy, he managed to pick up the earlier conversation. He'd thought it through the best he could.

"Bud, you use the money to head for the stars. Your mom was trapped. You go with your dreams, go for you, and her, and me too. Go wherever your heart calls you. Use her money as your own and take her precious memory with you. Honor her, and me, by you being all you can be. Promise me, Bud, promise me that you'll do it."

Bud was now crying too. "I promise, Dad, I do promise. I'll try to walk among the stars and find my way to the better places as God will lead. And, wherever that is, you and Mom will always be with me—and with each other!" They both smiled. No more words were needed.

Minutes passed. Bud finally spoke again, softly. Maybe it wasn't any of his business, and it really didn't make any difference now, but he just had to know. If his dad wouldn't tell him, that would be OK.

"There was a woman, Dad, she used to come to the marina to visit you. That caused some rumors in the village. Did you know that?"

"Woman? Oh, yeah. That's Maggie Welch. Her husband Herb and I served together in the war. He left her and then I think he might have died, I'm not sure. We talked when she came to my marina, Maggie and me. Yes, we did. We both needed to, and we didn't care if people talked behind our backs. Sometimes that can't be avoided."

"Sorry, Dad, to push this a little, but I need to know. Did you and this Maggie just talk?—the rumors took it further and hurt Mom and me." Bert had pain in his face, and not just from the awkward question.

"Help me move this leg, Bud, it hurts. I'm so stupidly helpless these days.... Thanks, that's better! Now about your question. Yeah, there were some secret connections involving Maggie and me, but not the kind that people like old Frank Halstead across the street used to think. Here's what I think—he was bored, kind of overpowered in life by his Hazel, and looked for something exciting he could spread around. Made him feel important, you know, to spice up the village a little. You and your mom paid some for that. I'm sorry. I could've stopped it."

"Yea, Dad, I sure agree. We paid a big price, and you could have stopped it if it weren't true. Do you want to tell now me about the real connections you had with Maggie or not?"

"Tell you now? Tell you the cold truth? Why not? It can't hurt Jess no more. But if you're thinking some juicy sex thing on the side, forget it, Son. Never was unfaithful to your mom, not like that anyway, not like Herb did to his Maggie. Truth is, Maggie and me were just really good friends, had been since before I met Jess and before Maggie and Herb got hitched. Their marriage was a hurried-up thing 'cause he and I were about to go to war. They weren't really ready and maybe shouldn't have done it, but they did, and it didn't last."

"So you all knew each other for a long time, and Mom was just squeezed into things later?"

"Something like that. Your mom surely felt squeezed alright, stuck where she wasn't quite wanted and didn't quite fit. We loved each other, mind you, but somehow that wasn't enough for her. After I got home from the Pacific, the four of us and you found our way out to this lake to start over—actually Herb had been hurt in the war, got home first, and they had come out here and let us know that we could come too when we

were ready. Well, we came and set up on opposite sides of the lake. Soon
that wasn't far enough away for your mom's comfort. Jess feared Maggie. She had suspicion stuck in her head—wasn't sure of herself, was
afraid of losing me, especially after Herb left Maggie and she was always
around and all alone."

"Why weren't you frank with Mom? You had nothing to hide."

"I tried to tell your mom it was OK, but I guess I've never been a
good talker. Maggie and I would talk sometimes, yeah, and I stayed
away from my home like I shouldn't have, I know, and your mom suf-
fered, sure did. I also know that I'm so sorry. Sure wish I could change
all that somehow, but some things can't be done, Son."

It was happening. Bud watched his dad crying, something he thought
he'd never see. How different from before. The weight of regret had gotten so heavy that the plugs in Bert's tear ducts had just popped out and
let the long-delayed flow come. It was like what must have happened
when the Lake Milton dam had first stopped the Mahoning River and the
land began submerging in the spreading water, with tree stumps and random debris slowly slipping out of sight. It was a lake of sorrow spilling
over Bert's face, a cleansing wash allowing the sadness of many yesterdays to find repentance in the glow of grace, and maybe a new beginning—right before the certain end.

Bud was crying too. Tears joined tears, making two men one. Bud
had never felt this close to his father. He decided on something he could
say to his dad, something that had needed to be said for a long time.

"Dad, I love you! I love you! Don't worry about the tears. They're
beautiful in their own strange way. Let me tell you something. I'm proud
to be your son!"

Bert seemed frozen, shocked in a wonderland where he hadn't been
before. Finally, he found some words and used what strength he had to
get them out.

"Well, I love you too Bud, always have. The worst thing is that I can't
change some things now. It's your mom. Dear Jess, we did love each
other and were happy, at least at first. Then she got stuck in the village. I
was hiding something big and bad, so I got lost in my own things where I
was comfortable. Maybe I kind of left her in a different way than Herb
left Maggie. I was always here, but not really here, not like I should have
been. I'm so sorry! I was so scared, always scared!"

Bert was weak to the point of barely being able to speak. It was at
least a gentler and more graceful immobility than it had been, a final
draining of strength, an approaching death that no longer could take this

man entirely away from his son. Bert had one question left for his son, and he managed to get it out.

"Bud, should I ask about that scar on your neck and burn mark on your hand? I've been way too removed from so much of your life, but I'm concerned about you. Are you OK?"

Yes, Bud was OK, and so pleased that his father was noticing and caring about him. He decided to answer without going into all that was involved. Time was short and this was hardly the most important subject they could address.

"The scar and splotch? There are stories involved, Dad, too long for now and not that important. Yea, I'm OK. The past has marked me, that's for sure. Even so, I'll be fine. And, Dad, I have a question for you. I've seen that eagle tattoo on your forearm many times. I've always assumed you got it overseas as a stamp of pride in your country. Right?"

"That's it, Son, pride, though my service had its downside, but, as you say, there's a story involved, too complicated and painful for now. We'll just ignore the negative side of the thing."

"If that's how you want it, Dad, but I've got to ask just one more thing. A couple of minutes ago I first noticed that silver cross around your neck. That's sure new, isn't it? What's its meaning for you?"

Bert's eyes moistened. Barely conscious now, he gathered what strength he had, obviously wanting to answer this question. He moved one hand slowly until it was on top of Bud's hand, flesh against flesh, heart reaching to heart.

"My friend Ed Sinclair got it for me, Bud. We talked lots and I asked him for it. When I go, I don't want to go alone. My special friend, he was on that cross for me!"

Their touching hands squeezed each other. Now they were real father and son—and they also were new brothers in faith!

Another minute passed. It was a beautiful silence, full and happy. Then Bert managed to ask yet another question.

"Have you ever married, son?" That question surprised Bud. The answer, however, was simple to give.

"No, Dad, I've been afraid. I've feared that I might not be the man that some woman deserved, and then she would sit at home and cry—and I couldn't stand that again."

"Yeah, I get it. Mostly my fault. Sorry...." He drifted away, and then came back, hoping to finish his thought, maybe his last.

"Do it boy; take the risk; love somebody like I did Jess at first. I tell you, do it boy! Use her—your--dream dollars. Go far away, not on the map necessarily, but away from the breakdowns and fears of yesterday.

Go out there among the stars; take somebody with you into life; make tomorrow different for both of you!"

Bert was gone again, hopefully not clear gone, but maybe. Bud had never heard such words from his dad's mouth. He wanted to understand why his dad had always been so afraid, and he wanted to respond with more understanding and gratitude, but he didn't get a chance.

That was it. Quiet took over again, and this time it didn't end with new talk. Bert did mumble something else once, "talk...Mike, ...help Mike... run from fear," or words close to those. Bud didn't know that they meant, if anything. He surely wanted nothing to do with the only Mike he could think of, that nasty kid from school days. And why warn against the danger of fear. He had never thought of his dad as being terribly afraid, not until now. Insensitive and self-preoccupied, sure, but not afraid. He knew his dad had grown to be frustrated and disappointed with his life, but truly afraid? Of what? Whatever had so frightened Bert was not going to stop Bud from moving on, however. With his dying breaths, Bert had tried to push his boy toward the future, full of faith and free of fear.

And then he was gone. The nurse was back in the room, checked a few things, and started turning off the machines. Bert Kraemer was finally pain free, fear free, fully at home where he always would be whole and surrounded by love. Bud hoped that Jessica would greet Bert with wild excitement, meet him somewhere out there in the great meeting place among the stars. Her man was sure ready to greet her, more than ready to regain love as it once had been and always ought to have been. And he'd left some marching orders for his son down here—who was so glad he'd come back home and gotten there just in time.

Bud would never forget those last simple words of his father, right before the mumbling that included the words "Mike" and "fear." They had been so loving, so affirming, so challenging. They were his permission for Bud to live! What were those marvelous words? Bud never intended to forget them. "Go out there among the stars and make tomorrow different!"

Bud stroked Bert's face gently. The blood had stopped moving and the harshness had seemed to soften. A liberated son spoke lovingly to his departed and liberated father, "I will, Dad, I will!!"

Chapter Sixteen

TURN THE KEY!

" "Turn the key, Son!" Those were among Bert Kraemer's last words. They had been directed straight into Bud's eyes by a dying man. Bert had tried in all his feebleness to release strength and resolve into his beloved boy. He wanted him to go daringly on with life, free of the shackles that had been hanging so heavy on the whole family, free to love, risk, and dream as his mother and father had failed to do so much of their lives.

Bert hadn't revealed the source of his own great fear. Bud wished he had—and he now remembered that StarWalker, many years before, had promised that Bud would understand someday. It didn't look like it now. No matter. The important things had been said and gotten done before the death, and that was enough.

The necessary call was made to the funeral home in nearby Newton Falls, the same one that Bud remembered had handled the final arrangements for his mother. There was an empty spot in the cemetery next to Jessica for her husband. Bud was sure that now she'd welcome having him that close to her forever—that's how she'd always wanted it. The "BJ" team was together again, finally.

It became Bud's responsibility to write a little obituary for the news-papers in Newton Falls, Warren, and Youngstown so that word could get out about the visiting hours if anyone were interested. Few likely would be. The service would be private. Things would be simple. Bud didn't know any preachers other than Ed Sinclair, the Baptist, in whose church he'd never been (nor had his dad as far as he knew). And Bud certainly wasn't inclined to call the priest of the local bingo-related parish.

The funeral home director said he could take care of things like that. Mostly, Bud just had to be there for the visiting hours to greet any visi-tors. There were lots of questions to answer and some faces from the past that might show. Bud, the only family member, would try to recognize people and be polite. He'd talk briefly and probably awkwardly with each as they tried to say something supportive and then head for the door, duty done. He didn't look forward to this time, but it was tradition-al, apparently necessary for the grieving business.

Bert had still owned the little house on Beach Lane. Should Bud keep or sell it? There also was the money box at the bank. What should he do with it? He had promised his dad in general, but without any particulars. He'd ponder the options and deal with the visitors and then figure it out.

As expected, there weren't many who showed up to pay their last re-spects. It's one price paid by a man who had isolated himself over the years, and a son who had abandoned the village for the bigger world. Maggie Welch was an exception. She was there as soon as the doors were opened to visitors. Bud didn't have to fumble for words in this case—this was a special woman to his dad, and not a rival for his mother after all. She came up to Bud, crying, glancing at Bert's neatly presented body dressed in a blue suit and a tie, hardly like him.

"I'm Maggie Welch. I knew your dad nearly all my life. He was a much better man than most folks ever got a chance to realize. I hope you know that. He and my Herb were friends too. That was a long time ago and you wouldn't know him, but the war did something to my man and I lost him to another woman. Your dad was hurt by the war too, but at least he knew how to be faithful—and he was always my friend, and no more despite the rumors over the years."

That was quite an opening speech, but people are awkward in a cir-cumstance like this and sometimes ramble out of nervousness.

"Hello, Mrs. Welch. Dad said some really kind things about you just before his death. Mom was afraid of you, I knew that even as a boy, but for no real reason apparently. Dad was so sorry for allowing that to go on. He said he was just too scared to face whatever was involved—he never got around to telling me what that was."

"Well, Bud, I stayed away from your mom because I feared she'd misunderstand, but I guess she did anyway. I'm so sorry about that. Jessica painted herself into a corner of suspicion and jealousy. Almost nobody else understood but me why your wonderful father was like he was—closed and scared, I mean. Something in Bert just couldn't be faced, and he wouldn't deal with it. He just looked the other way and let it be. Yes, Bud, he was afraid, very afraid. But both of your parents are at peace now. I hope you can find yours too. Your dad would surely want you to."

Bud wasn't sure what to say to all of this—some of which he had heard from his dad. All that came out of his mouth was, "Thanks, Mrs. Welch, thanks for your friendship with Dad. This leaves you so alone now, your man and your friend both gone. Will you be OK?"

Maggie was so pleased that Bud wasn't upset with her and was even concerned about her well being. She tried to assure him and then went on her way, leaving Bud with that big question his dad never answered. What exactly was Bert so afraid of? He wished he'd asked Maggie directly since she seemed to know, but she might not have told him either, partly because of time. A few others had now come into the room and were waiting respectfully on Maggie to be done. Now she was gone and another woman was walking up to Bud.

"Hello, Mr. Kraemer. I'm Joan Howard—you once knew me as Miss Mason when you were in school."

"Miss Mason! Hello. What a great surprise."

I'm so sorry for your loss, Bud, and so proud of who you've become. Of course, I knew about your leaving Craig Beach after you graduated. After all, I urged you to do it. You were a little like that George who left Winesburg, Ohio. Do you remember that novel I once had you read?"

"I'm sorry, I missed your new name, oh, yes, Mrs. Howard. And I sure do remember that novel. And yes, I did leave Craig Beach and, mostly because of your encouragement. I've become an English literature teacher. I'll always be in your debt. Have you left here too and gotten married?"

"Yes, but not out of frustration with the little school in Pricetown. I met Mr. Howard at a teacher's meeting. Eventually we married and I moved to Warren to be with him. I teach over there now and am very happy. But I've never forgotten you, or your dear mother. I sat with her sometimes when she was so ill."

"I know you did. Thanks for that, Mrs. Howard. Her name was Jessica, and you're an angel!"

"Hardly an angel, Bud, but it does sound good! One more thing and then I'll hurry along. Your mother confided in me more than once. She was scared and jealous, and she so loved you with everything in her. She loved your dad, too, really loved him, but felt she'd lost him, so she was lost too. That must have hurt both of them deeply, and, of course, you also. In one way, I'm glad it's over for your father—he was caught in a tangled web of life and this apparently was his best way out. Forgive me if I shouldn't say something like that."

Bud teared up—he'd promised himself he wouldn't do that, no matter what, not in front of these people, but this was more than he could handle. He was embarrassed in front of his former teacher, but she moved quickly to soften the blow. Smiling gently at him, she took his hands in hers and tried to set him at ease.

"It's alright for tears to come today, Bud. When you were a schoolboy, you needed to cry sometimes and you fought them off. I felt so sorry for you. But that was yesterday." And so it was; it was quite a different day and he let the tears come.

"I only wish I could have talked candidly with you many years ago, Bud. I might have saved you some pain, but back then it just wasn't my place to interfere." She embraced him tenderly—the first time any woman other than his mother had ever held him like that. It felt so good! He finally got hold of himself and thanked her for her gifts to his life, and to his mother's, including the gift of coming on this sad day.

She smiled again, wished him well, and stepped away to allow others their chance to speak to Bud. A man was now right behind Mrs. Howard, someone Bud didn't know. This could be awkward.

"So you're Bud Kraemer? I'm Gerald from the local tavern in Craig Beach. In the last couple of years your dad would stop by for a beer or two and some good talk. Good guy. Lonely, scared, actually kind of hoped for this day. Good to see him resting. Where'd he get that tie? Never saw him dressed up like that."

"I had to buy it from the funeral home. I don't think we ever met, but thanks for coming."

"Sure. Best wishes to you. Your dad was a hell of a man! See you sometime if you're back around this way."

That came out of nowhere for Bud. So his dad had reached out some for companionship, tavern or not. Good for him. Bud was comforted by his assurance that Bert, this "hell of a man," had headed far away from hell when he finally died!

"Thanks for coming, Gerald, and for your friendship to Dad." Both smiled and Gerald moved over, glancing at the body quickly, obviously not comfortable in this place. At least he had come.

The next person in line was recognized immediately. It was Delores, a good friend from school days, the one who lived near the mysterious pond and once had her foot bitten by the dragon that may or may not have even existed. He was delighted to see her! She was married now, she told him, had lost a child some years back (not to the dragon, Bud presumed), and was still living in the village, but not right next to the pond anymore. She seemed sadder than anyone about Bert's death and told Bud that her husband had been a regular at Bert's marina when it was still open. He and Bert had been good buddies.

"Wonderful, Delores. Why isn't he here too? I'd like to meet and thank him. Do I know him?"

"Yes, you do, Bud, and that's why he didn't want to face you. I'm sure you remember Mike Jakas, the nasty kid. You used to say behind his back that his last name reminded you of a particular beast of burden—you'd have been in trouble if your mom had ever heard you actually say that "...ass" word, and he'd have taken your head off if he'd ever heard you use it. Well, anyway, he's my husband now—think of that, Delores Jakas!"

He had trouble keeping his mouth from dropping open. "Really?" She smiled, not surprised at his shock, and obviously had more that needed to be said. Bud was all ears.

"Back in school days Mike was hard on you sometimes, Bud, not kind to say the least. He's ashamed and very embarrassed now, I can tell you that for sure, and he apologized to your dad more than once for how he treated you. He's particularly sorry for what he once said about your mom in front of the kids on the school bus. He might have tried to apologize to you too, but he'd lost track of you. So you understand that he just couldn't come here. Please forgive him."

Bud had to get his thoughts and emotions organized. Finally, he said, "It's this way, Delores. I do remember him alright, and not so kindly, as you would guess. Actually, I wish we could meet and patch up old times. Leaving it alone is not good for either of us. If he really is sorry and a different person, I could manage to forgive him. After all, any buddy of my dad is potentially mine too. And he must have reformed or someone like you could never live with him. He's being good to you, I hope."

"He is, and he'll be so glad to hear of your forgiving spirit. Mike and your dad hit it off real well. How long are you going to be back here? He'd be willing to meet you, I'm sure, but not in front of other people. He said he owes you an ice cream cone—remember Sinclair's store after the park fire? In fact, he has a little business deal he wants to propose to you if he gets a chance."

"I'll be around for a couple of days, and a business deal—can I assume that it's not a dirty deal, or maybe a bribe? A sincere apology would be enough—no money required!" They both laughed quietly. Then he added something of a much more serious nature.

"By the way, Delores, I just remembered something. My dad's last words included some mumbling about a Mike. Now I think I might know who he meant. I'll bet he wanted a Jakas-Kraemer meeting. Maybe he even knew in advance about whatever business Mike has on his mind."

"He might have. Mike would walk down to the marina sometimes. He always bought his bait there for his Saturday morning fishing trips on the lake. He and your dad talked lots—it had to be at Gerald's Tavern after your dad's marina closed. They were kind of pals, both a little rough around the edges, but very warm if you get deep enough. I've gotten real deep with Mike, trust me, Bud, so I know he's not planning to do you in!"

"Tell you what, Delores. I finally got that deep with my dad, too, at least for a few minutes, and I'm so thankful. I must visit Mike, for my dad's sake if for no other reason. I need to know about this deal he has in mind and find out if he's got another black eye waiting for me. And if he really has changed, tell him that he owes me an ice cream cone—a big one!"

Delores smiled, relieved that this tarnished past might get polished a little and then the guys could work out their business as friends. She said she'd get Mike in touch right away. She wrote down the phone number of the little place where Bud was staying.

"He wants to apologize, he really does, Bud, and then tell you about a hope he has—this deal. I'll give you a little heads up. He wants to buy another house in the village to use as a rental for some extra income. Maybe you'll have one for sale soon and would be willing to come to some agreement."

"So that's it. Well, maybe, I haven't thought much about that yet. I assume he's meaning my home place, but I'm certainly not going to live there. We'll talk and see."

That was it. Delores wanted to hurry home to share the news. She was excited and glad. Bud thought at first that no one else would come and this visiting thing could be over. His conversations had been surprisingly good. But, no, the door opened again. It was Rev. Ed Sinclair, and behind him Betsy. He hadn't thought about seeing Betsy again—this might make the whole time worthwhile! The old man approached first with the one arm of his suit jacket hanging empty. He looked in the casket for an unusually long time, was obviously very sad at this death, and then walked over to Bud. Even though Bud was more anxious to talk to Betsy, she sat down to wait patiently until Mr. Sinclair had his turn.

"Welcome home, Bud. God will be with you in this thing. Death is hard, but it's not the end. Hold on to faith. Bert finally found some of his own. He told me about it personally, even came to my church a little toward the end." He reached out to embrace Bud, a bit awkward with one arm. Bud was quite surprised and pleased to hear that his dad had gone to church, even just a little. That was sure different.

"I see that someone else is waiting to talk to you, Bud. What I have to say may take longer than what we have here. Please come to my church tomorrow around noon and we'll finish there—can you do that? It's important. You remember where it is, opposite Craig Beach on the Youngstown side of the lake."

"Yeah, I suppose, Mr. Sinclair. I've never been to your church, but I know where it is. So you need to talk to me about what?"

"Really do, son. Let's leave it to tomorrow. See you then around noon."

That was almost as surprising as the Mike Jakas thing, and a little more mysterious. But apparently it would have to wait. Rev. Sinclair already had stepped aside and Bud's mind shot elsewhere when he looked into Betsy's face. She sure was a lovely woman and there were many good memories.

"Hi, Bud, it's been such a long time!" His eyes sparkled. He hoped she hadn't seen that—he was embarrassing himself. This was a special moment for him, whether or not it should have been. She hadn't come in with a husband, so he had felt a little freedom to indulge himself. She kept talking, a good thing since it gave him time to focus his thoughts and control his emotions.

"Sorry I didn't really know your dad, Bud, but I sure remember you." Since no one else but the funeral director was now in the building, Bud and Betsy sat down together and began to talk freely. Betsy shared her sorrow at Bud's loss and, since she seemed to be in no hurry, he asked about her life.

"How have things gone for you over the years since school?"

"It's not been the best, Bud, not what I had hoped. You might remember that my dad drank way too much and sometimes hit my mom. I was always so afraid that someone would find out and he'd get mad at me for telling."

"I do remember about that. You must have told me about it once. We did share our problems occasionally."

"I did. I remember. It was a very big thing for me to risk telling anybody. You were the only one in the school that I thought would appreciate my awkward circumstance and keep your mouth shut. I just had to tell somebody! And you will remember that sometimes you would talk to me about your mom crying and being so unhappy."

"Sure I remember, Betsy. We both had big problems at home, didn't we? You were about the only bright spot I had in life. Thanks for having been there for me!" She smiled and decided to tease him a little.

"What about the Hutchins place, Bud? I remember that you got your haircut there more often than necessary just because you always hoped to see Shirley—I'll bet you remember her!"

He was a bit embarrassed. "Well, Betsy, you got me there. Nobody could forget Shirley! I liked how she could make me laugh. I admit it. But there's one difference, a big one. You made me feel warm and good and OK deep inside. I loved you for that!"

Betsy became quiet, even a little flushed, so the teasing was over. What a beautiful sentiment had come out of Bud. Even so, he was sorry he had used the word "loved." Still, it had come out and he'd let it stand.

"Pleased to have done that for you, Bud, but there's more to share about my life if you really want to hear all this stuff." They had the time, the funeral director seemed in no hurry at all, and no one else was showing up to visit. Why not?

Betsy was amazingly frank. "Bud, I've been so stupid. My dad eventually died—I think the drink finally killed him. Mom is still with us, and was so upset when later I decided to marry. The problem was that the guy I fell in love with also had a drinking problem. You know how some abused women do. I was sure my case was different. I would so love him that he would get past his drinking one day. Well, he didn't. The short of it is that a most unpleasant divorce became necessary. I don't even know where he is anymore, and I don't care. At least we didn't have any children who would have to suffer with our sad situation. I duplicated my dad by choosing my husband, and in the process doubled my mom's misery and my own. Ever since the divorce, and I'm sure you could understand, I've been afraid of close relationships."

Bud just looked at her, so sad to hear about all this misery, so understanding of the fear of human intimacy. After all, that was about his situation too. He'd admitted exactly that to his dad before he died. What had Bert then said to him? It had been something like, "Turn the key, Son, open tomorrow and risk walking right in." Given all she'd said, Bud decided to share something with Betsy.

"Betsy, my dad on his dying day gave me some advice. What he meant basically was something like this. "I cut you and your mom off from my inner life, and we all became the losers. Don't you go and do the same thing! Risk loving even if you haven't seen it modeled well.""

Just saying this out loud kind of shocked Bud. It was like a SkyWalker moment for him, a daring burst of clarity coming in a very different kind of setting. And now, there lay his dad, quiet and cold, at least in appearance not that different from his real life. From that coldness, however, Bud was hearing the call to a life of human warmth and honest sharing and risk taking. It was a last gift from his father—and a most precious one! Bud looked at his dad lying there, so dead and yet somehow not altogether.

Betsy broke this strange silence, pulling Bud's gaze back her way. "Are you OK, Bud? You got so quiet there, like you were in a world of your own."

"Sorry, I guess I was, Betsy. It was a little wave of grief for my dad, a little pondering about something he'd said to me." Bud didn't say anything more to her about what his dad's advice, but he marveled at how at ease he was in her presence. So he decided to say one more thing to her. He would refuse to live in fear, be another ice-man. He glanced again at his dad's face, so still and serene now, but somehow still counseling his son from the other side. Bud was sure he could see just a glimpse of a faint smile. Finally!

He took a risk. "Betsy, I'll be here for a couple of days. I need to go and see Mike Jakas, remember him? And pastor Ed Sinclair too—I know you'd recall him from down at the store. I think I know what to do with the old house on Beach Lane, and I have to finish a little banking I'm left with. Could I add you to my to-do list? Could we meet again before I leave, maybe for dinner or something? That would mean a lot to me."

He watched her face closely, afraid she'd say no. He really wanted her to say "Yes!" And he was sorry that he had put her at the end of his "to-do list." What a dumb thing to say to a woman! That might have made her sound secondary—and she wasn't, never had been, not to him!

"Well, Bud, since you've asked, OK. I think I would like that, I really would. I'll arrange for a friend to sit with mom and that way we can have a whole evening if you want it." He really did. He reached out and took her hand. He held it gently, with her noticing the red splotch on the back of his, and his noticing that there was just a touch of fresh red on her face.

"I'll be in touch, and really look forward to it!" She smiled and politely left the room. Bud said under his breath, walking back over to the casket, "Well, Dad, you said to turn the key. I'm trying. Who knows if any door will open for me. At least, I hope St. Peter has swung wide open heaven's gate for you!"

The key was turning, at least a little. It was the key that unlocks new emotions, honest vulnerability, maybe even love. Bud was reaching out, risking, connecting, reconciling—apparently even with big, bad Mike. He wasn't sure what Pastor Ed had in mind, but he was a good man, so that wasn't any concern, just an interesting mystery.

Bud's head and heart were unusually full. Dad was gone and he'd made it to his side in time. The biggest question now was, "Could love actually be possible for myself, real love with a woman, with genuine trust and full of self-giving and honest communication?" He'd never seen such a thing in action close up and wasn't sure he would know how to do it. The very idea was scary, but very attractive nonetheless.

However that all was or would be, Bud just loved Betsy's sweet little smile and very kind heart—and it was getting hard to think about much else. He turned toward the casket one final time. A small spray of flowers had been placed across Bert's waist. Bud had arranged for that and chosen the words printed in gold on the attached ribbon. He read them again, and then found himself saying them aloud.

"THANKS, DAD!" That was all, but that was so much! Next to these words were two hearts. Inside one was "BJ." Inside the other was "BB." It seemed so right to link his mom and dad that way again, and for the first time to link his dad and himself so intimately. And then it hit him.

"Can you believe it! 'BB' could also have another meaning. Bud's dinner with Betsy was tomorrow evening. He could hardly wait that long.

Chapter Seventeen

STOP! STOP!

Funerals are never fun, but this one was as comfortable as Bud Kraemer could arrange. It was very simple and completely private. It was out at the local cemetery next to the plot where his mother was buried. Bud had asked the funeral director to come with him, bring a Bible, read and say a few traditional things, and that was it. The comments ended with a reading of the Lord's Prayer from the New Testament. Bud heard more clearly than ever before the ending words, "for Thine is the kingdom and the power and the glory forever. Amen."

"Amen indeed!" Bud repeated these words aloud as he looked at the coldness of the hole in the ground. "Not much of the power and glory stuff lies on our human side of things. But our side isn't the only one!"

Bud walked away thanking the funeral director and thinking some more. This was the first of all future days without his father. The funeral clearly was a forever event. Life and death make obvious that people are so fragile and often fickle, so short-lived and unworthy in themselves of any ultimate praise. So, that was it.

Then came the next day and the promised meetings with Mike Jakas and Ed Sinclair and, of course, with Betsy for dinner. It wasn't clear what all might come from these meetings, so Bud got right to it. Things began with a delicate but good reconciliation with Mike Jakas. These two boys, now mature men, were done with bouts of slander and days of humiliation. They finally accepted each other as equals.

A business deal with Mike could be worked out. Selling Mike and Delores the home on Beach Lane made good sense to all of them. Mike wanted it as an investment property and was willing to put some money into its repair and upkeep. He was sure that better economic days were coming for Craig Beach and he wanted to be ahead of the curve. Beyond that, Bud felt really good about the idea of his boyhood home being refreshed for the future. He also liked having that mean kid, now a much-mellowed man, apologizing sincerely for past actions that had been wholly uncalled for. He teased Mike, certainly a first.

"Your penance for the past is for you to take great care of my home forever! Otherwise, I'll...."

"Don't finish that sentence, Bud. You might say something to mess everything up for us. And about the house and its care, you got it kid—I mean, 'Yes, Sir!'"

Delores was so happy that these guys, both important in her life, had buried the hatchet, and not in each other's skulls! If there were any Indians being massacred in the nearby woods, as Bud once claimed there actually were, they'd surely be glad to hear the good news. At least in the village, war paint had turned into a peace pipe.

Now it would be on to Ed Sinclair's place across the lake. Bud had that appointment too and the time had come. The church was even smaller inside than Bud had expected. No matter. He had driven straight there from Mike and Delores' place. Ed was waiting for him and had more to share than Bud could have imagined. The door opened before Bud even got to it—Ed was anxious!

"Thanks for coming, Bud. Come in and sit down over here—he pointed to where two chairs were close together. A soft drink or coffee maybe?"

"No thanks, just had some at the Jakas home. You likely don't remember them—classmates of mine I was reconnecting with. And your wife, Joyce wasn't it?"

"Bud, it was Joyce, and like your mom, she died much too young."

"Sorry to hear that. I'll never forget the day she arranged for me to get a free ice cream cone at your store, and without getting me beat up by Mike Jakas, the guy who's suddenly now my friend."

"Sounds like Joyce, and since you're here in one piece, fresh from the Jakas place, I can see that some peace has been made. We need more of that in this world."

"It sure has, Rev. Sinclair. Feels good too. Now to what's on your mind. I'm curious and have absolutely no idea."

"Sure, I know it's out of the blue. It was just too much to talk about at the funeral home. Let me begin, Bud, by telling you this. Your dad and I were close friends for many years. I deeply mourn his loss. We talked many times, and sometimes about pretty serious things. I'll never forget one Sunday afternoon when Maggie Welch and I went to your dad's marina to confront him with what we had learned from Herb, Maggie's ex-husband. I don't think you've ever met him."

"I've heard the name, but that's all."

"You were there that day, Bud, but left to help your mother with something before the serious talking started. We deliberately waited until you were gone and then dumped the truth on your dad. It was nothing he didn't know, but stuff he just didn't want to face and do anything about. He responded about how we expected he would. He tried to duck us, tried hard not face what we had to say, but we didn't back off. We were sure we needed to push hard. We did, and still we didn't get him to agree with us. He was just so afraid!"

"What did you want him to agree with that he already knew? I know Dad was afraid, but he died without ever telling me why."

"That's not surprising, Bud. Maggie and I insisted that he should tell your mom, and maybe you too, tell you everything about what happened years before, what had him so afraid. But he was a strong and extremely proud man—and full of this big fear that you and your mom never understood. Now he's gone, and your dear mom too, and I want you to know the facts after all this time. I think Bert would want you to know now. He has nothing to fear anymore."

"Know what? What was he afraid of, Rev Sinclair? Did he live a double life that Mom and I never knew about—Mom always feared that he did?"

"Well, Son, he did in a way, but definitely not in the way you might think or your mom feared, not anything like Maggie's Herb did with another woman. It's just that Bert had a very bad memory from something that happened during the war and he hid it all the rest of his life, so scared that his family would find out."

"Dad and I had a good talk before he died, but he never mentioned some bad memory. He was being pretty up-front with me. Please go ahead and tell me about it. I know you and trust that you will tell me the truth, and out of good motivation. I have to know the truth, Rev. Sinclair."

"Son, here it is. Killing is what war is all about. You've known all your life that I have a missing arm. One of my own friends was careless on the firing range and hit me by accident. I was a victim of friendly fire. I got a purple heart and was sent home—I think he did too, but without the honor. My wound shows, and there is nothing for me to be ashamed of. Not so with your dad, or so he thought. No one could see his big wound."

"OK, I had wondered what happened to your arm, but let's get right to it. What happened to Dad, and in a way he thought he had to be ashamed of?"

"Well, Bud, the moment came, and came very suddenly, when your dad had to kill. He was on regular deck security duty on his ship when it happened. And this is where the heart of his fear came from, Bud, not just what happened, but how it happened. He was so afraid that you and your mom would hold it against him if you ever knew. The two of you might even have become afraid of him because of it. So he never told you despite how much it bothered him."

"Rev. Sinclair, please get specific. What happened?"

"What happened poisoned your family life ever after, and it shouldn't have, needn't have. Your dad misjudged the response you and your mom would have if he told you about it—he thought you might think he would do it again, even to one of you. He was wrong. He paid a big price for his silence, his fear, his misjudgment, and so did both of you—and even Maggie Welch who had to avoid your mom because of her jealously."

Bud seemed to have no words, only wide open ears. But he was getting impatient. This frustrating thought crossed his mind—"Do all preachers go on and on before they get to the bottom line?"

"Rev. Sinclair, please tell me exactly what Dad did that caused him such a long-term fear."

"It's very simple, Bud. He killed a man, a Japanese soldier barely eighteen years old. He was a prisoner being held below decks on your dad's ship. Somehow the man had gotten free. He found his way up to where your dad was on watch. Bert was all alone on a poorly lighted deck bobbing in a troubled sea. Then it happened. It suddenly was hand-to-hand, not pretty, death for the prisoner, but a death necessary for the safety of the wartime ship and your dad's crewmates. Then, for all the rest of his years, Bert let that one incident of war control and even destroy his life."

"So Dad killed a young man with his bare hands? I never knew that, not even a hint!"

"I know. Actually, it wasn't his bare hands. He used the knife he carried and could reach more quickly than his firearm. In a flash, it became for him a blade of destiny that cut one throat and then ripped the heart out of the cutter. The fact is that your dad, in all his apparent insensitivity over the years, was a very sensitive man indeed. He felt guilty, even dirty and unworthy of you and your mom. He finally convinced himself that he might do it again, get violent if adequately provoked—silly, I'm sure, not really a possibility, especially not against those he loved so deeply, but he let that fear fill him enough to paralyze him emotionally."

Ed reached into a drawer. He had something to show and then give Bud. "Here, Bud, this is the little medal that the Navy awarded your father for his bravery and service to the ship's endangered crew that fateful day. Bert gave it to me years ago because he was afraid you'd find it by accident some day if he kept it anywhere around the house. It belongs to you now. I hope you will keep it with pride."

Bud sat very still, imagining not only that ugly ship scene but also that serene smile that was his last memory of his father's face. His heart cried out—"Dad, I know now and it's OK!!"

Mr. Sinclair was still talking. "Bert loved you and Jessica way too much to risk anything going wrong. So he hid his medal and real self from you, even isolated himself physically from you much of the time. He paid a great price, as I said, and so did you and your mom. I'm so sorry, and so was he! That's just the way it was. I thought you deserved to know, Bud."

"Thanks, thanks so much for telling me all this! By the way, how did you learn about it, Mr. Sinclair, all directly from Dad?"

"Well, Herb Welch, who had been on that ship with your dad, told his wife Maggie years ago before he left her, and eventually she shared it with me, her pastor, when she saw your father struggling so much. We finally let Bert know that we knew, and tried to get him to tell you and your mom, but it didn't change anything. He just couldn't."

Bud fumbled with the precious medal, shiny and strange looking next to the red splotch on the back of his hand. So he and his dad both carried scars from violent yesterdays. He caressed the medal lovingly. Words strained to come out of his mouth—they'd already formed in his heart. When they came, they were few, and Bud wasn't embarrassed to let them out right in front of another man. He looked up at the ceiling as though he was speaking directly to his father.

"I love you, Dad!! I'm so sorry for the great pain of your years. Mom and I would have understood, I know we would have, and we would have been proud. You should have told us! No matter. Now I know, and somehow she probably does too."

He and Ed looked into each others eyes, all filled with tears. The men embraced, a total of three arms sharing relief and gratitude. Ed said only this and then he was done.

"Guilt and fear are terrible things, Son. Your dad kept looking *inside* and couldn't find freedom. I encourage you to look *upward* and be free!" Bud nodded. He understood and agreed completely.

Well, it was time to leave—any more time and maybe Ed would have turned Bud into a handclapping and shouting Baptist! Before he could clear the door, however, the phone rang. Ed answered and almost immediately motioned for Bud to wait. After a few comments back and forth with the caller, Ed hung up.

"Bud, please come back and sit down. We have a surprise visitor coming. It's Herb Welch, Maggie's ex! I haven't seen him for years and I don't think Maggie has either. Actually, I thought he was dead--I don't know what she assumes, and we're not going to alert her to his coming. It's only you he desperately wants to see."

"Why me? I know Dad's story now. Is this necessary? I don't want to go through the story again."

"I told him you already knew, but he says it's really important, Bud. Please stay. Herb was your dad's close buddy on that war ship. He saw the obituary in the Youngstown paper but deliberately didn't go to the funeral home. He figured Maggie would be there and his presence might cause an unpleasant scene. He was hoping that you were still in town. Bud, he's only five minutes away and is rushing here to see you. I think it's very important and I want you to wait."

They both sat down, quiet and confused, and a little nervous. What could this possibly be about? Soon a knock at the door brought into the room an old man with a serious look on his face. Herb also was shown a seat. It was near Bud. Herb was the first to speak.

"So you're Bert's boy? Thanks for waiting on me. Where should I begin? Well, I'm the guy who joined up with your dad. We shipped out together right into the teeth of that terrible war. We were always together, and naturally we were on the same ship that awful day that I need to tell you about. May I go on, Bud?"

"Yes, of course, if you want to. But you need to know that Ed's already told me what happened and you don't have to go through that painful business again. And thanks for being a good friend to Dad. I wish I had known him back then. I do have some letters he wrote to Mom from the sea, letters that reveal much about him. I now treasure those letters, and this little metal of his too." He pulled it from his pocket and showed it to Herb.

"Well, son, the medal's nice, well deserved, and I've seen it before. But I do have to tell again the story of what happened because I'm sure that the version you got is only part of the truth. You see, I never told Maggie the whole thing, I just couldn't, and what Ed told you had to come from Maggie." Now Bud was really listening!

"There's more?"

"Yes, there sure is. By the way, you say you have letters from your dad? Did he say anything about that day and my role in it?" Herb suddenly looked worried.

"No, he doesn't mention you or that day. I know nothing except what Mr. Sinclair told me a few minutes ago, what Maggie had told him. What else is there?"

Herb was obviously uncomfortable, like a little boy caught red-handed and about to be punished. "It's this way. Your dad, Bud, never knew himself what really happened!! I'm the only one who knows, and now I've got to get it off my chest!"

"What? Are you saying you're the one who killed that young man and not Dad? How would he not have known that?"

"I wish that were the truth, Son, but it isn't. I didn't kill anybody. Bert killed that boy alright, quick and sure, just as he had to. But that's not the point. He did it *because of me*! Bert never even suspected, never did in his whole life, but the whole thing was really *my fault*. I need to tell this and have somebody finally forgive me, if that's possible!"

Bud and Ed were silent, having no idea what was coming next. Why would Herb blame himself for what Bert had done? Maybe the old man wasn't thinking rationally anymore. But a little more from Herb and there'd be no doubt that he was thinking clearly indeed.

"I made a stupid little mistake below decks and that's how that Jap got loose in the first place. I should have gone up on deck immediately and tracked him down, sounded the alarm, alerted the watch on duty to be ready to subdue the man wherever he showed. But I was embarrassed and scared because of my stupidity. So I stayed below for two or three minutes to cover my tracks, being sure the escape wouldn't be blamed on me. Then I was going up after him. In the meantime, the prisoner had time to sneak around up on deck. He must have run into your dad suddenly, Bud, rushed at him, and your dad took care of the matter for me.

That's the rest of the story no one has ever known, including your dad. *I made it necessary for Bert to kill that Jap kid!*"

The room was very quiet now. Finally, Ed asked, "Do you know any more of the details, Herb? Is that everything?"

"Yea, I do know some more. The lookout on the mast above Bert reported later that he saw it all. He said the Jap had grabbed a hammer or something like that and charged at your dad. That was a mistake, the last for the young Oriental. Bert's training and survival instinct took over. His knife flashed and there was one less prisoner." Silence returned to the room, broken finally by Ed again since Bud appeared speechless.

"Herb, you've done a good thing by coming here today. Confession is good for a man's soul. What's it been like carrying this story all alone for these many years?" Herb was willing to answer, although he really wanted to know how Bud was taking this big news. Bud was just looking at the floor trying to process what he had heard.

"It's been pure hell! I couldn't live with myself, and not with Maggie either. After that terrible day on the ship, I wasn't the man she'd married and I couldn't face it. How do you tell a woman something like that, and how do you live with her if you don't tell her? Well, finally I left and have been running ever since, a little like Bert did. He didn't leave, just shut out his beloved Jessica—Maggie told me about that before we quit communicating years ago. Knowing that about Bert killed me all over again, but I just couldn't bring myself to do anything about it. I guess he couldn't either."

Bud finally was ready to say something. "So, Maggie became another victim of the war, as you are, Herb, and also Dad and Mom and me, all of us because two men were guilt-ridden victims over the same thing, and nobody would face the truth as they knew it? And the real truth is that my dad was anything but an aggressive killer like he feared, just a guy caught in an impossible situation thrown right in his face by you? Do I have that all right, Herb?"

Herb was now scared, ready for Bud to damn him to hell. "You have it about right, Son. I'm so ashamed! I should have yelled, 'STOP! STOP!' and thrown the alarm and pursued that man before he ever got up on deck with a weapon in his hands and anywhere near your dad. But I didn't. I froze. I let somebody clean up my mess. That's all. I just didn't! And then neither Bert nor I could face what each of us knew. We couldn't tell anybody or live normally anymore. That war isn't over yet!"

The three men looked at each other. What now? For Bud, there seemed to be no point in going after a broken old man who was sobbing with repentance. Bud's mind went instead to his dad. He'd seen a whole new dad when he first read those letters from sea, and now he'd just seen a whole new dad again!

Ed was thinking now as a pastor, deeply worried about Herb. He raised a question, delaying the response from Bud that Herb was fearing. "Herb, shouldn't Maggie be told all this? Maybe one person can still be saved. She lives only minutes away. Isn't there some way that you and Maggie could repair all these broken years between you? She has a for-giving heart. Despite what she's assumed all this time, you're saying that your running away from her wasn't just another woman you picked over her—just knowing that much would be so meaningful to her. I know Maggie well, I'm her pastor. Please help her."

"You do what you want about telling her—I've no reputation left to be hurt. I still do love her, so if telling her would help, do it. But I can't, can't anymore than Bert could tell his Jessica. Tell Maggie I'm a coward, but be sure to add that neither Bert nor I were ever killers at heart. I have another family now—didn't start the best way, but were managing and that's how it'll stay. You can tell Maggie for me that I wish so much that it had all been very different! Life is what it is, and that's all."

Then Herb looked right at Bud, having to know his response. He said to him, "At least I couldn't pass up this chance to tell you, Bud. It's one little gift I could give my friend Bert—and I owe him so much!" When Bud didn't respond immediately, he panicked and walked toward the door. Bud was trying to think of what he should say. He had to say some-thing, and quickly.

"Herb, wait a minute." Herb stopped, looked at Bud, and slumped in a chair close to the door. He was ready to take his medicine. Bud's voice was surprisingly calm.

"First, thanks so much for coming! You've filled in the picture of the past and that's so important to me. I admit it. I want very much to hate you. But that's no good. And given Dad's attitudes and new faith before he died, I'll say this to you on his behalf. He would have forgiven you, I know he would've. It sounds like both of you reacted to something you never wanted, found things in yourselves that weren't the best, and didn't have the strength to deal with it in ways that would have kept it from hurting the rest of us."

Herb sat motionless and listened like his life depended on every word. Bud continued.

"We're all human, Herb, all of us have sinned, and, as I know Pastor Sinclair here would want you to know, we're all candidates for God's forgiveness. So let me be the first to forgive—and it comes to you through me by way of God. Without his first forgiving me for many things, I wouldn't have the grace to forgive you."

These amazing words put some color back into Herb's whitened face. He began crying and came slowly to his feet and headed the few steps toward Bud. He had his arms out to embrace Bert's boy and, as much as he could, to even embrace Bert through his dear Bud. The tender embrace of a weakened but liberated man was emotional and was followed another comment. It was Herb's heart bleeding and healing at the same time.

"Those are the kindest words I've ever heard, Bud! Please, Ed, help Maggie find some good in all this if you can. Maybe there is a good God after all. Now I'd better really go, but I'm so glad I came!"

Herb Welch walked to his car and it was over—and yet something brand new had just begun, certainly for Bud, and maybe even for Herb and Maggie in their separate worlds. If Bert and Jessica hadn't been comfortably at rest before this hour at Pastor Sinclair's, they surely were now.

Bud had to absorb all this and also try to remember what else he was supposed to do today—and he was already late! Betsy was still on tap for dinner, but the planned schedule was now way off. He called her from Ed's to confess that he knew what time it was and that he was emotionally shaken from things he had just learned about his father and the war. He'd explain it all when they got together.

"Tell you what, Bud," said Betsy. "I can hear your voice trembling. It must have been something pretty big. I'm willing to delay our dinner until tomorrow evening. Sounds like you need a little private time and some sleep, and I'd like a full evening together if we can. So let's delay dinner. Can we do that? Will you still be here tomorrow?"

"Yes Betsy. I'll be here one more day. Maybe the delay would be best—and I'm really looking forward to our time together." She was so thoughtful, and he loved that positive note in her voice! Could life really turn in a direction not shrouded in darkness from the past? Maybe.

Chapter Eighteen

FINAL FLIGHT

The next day was a pretty one. The sky was clear and the lake water as smooth as glass. Was this a sign of the future, or only a lull before some new storm? Life doesn't come with such questions pre-answered. Bud hadn't slept well. Despite having forgiven Herb Welch with images of that ship incident kept flying around in his head. Since his business at the bank and with Mike Jakas were cared for, he decided to take a walk and think in the quiet of the morning, maybe mostly dreaming about the coming evening with Betsy. So much was happening. So much was different and still unknown.

Bud had a great idea. Why not visit Morning Glen one last time? Where better to think and anticipate? After all, somebody might buy these woods and cut the big trees down. Maybe the Youngstown man who once had owned the park now owned the woods. If that guy knew that Bert Kraemer once suggested that the fire at the park's bowling alley was the fault of his lack of maintenance, and that his boy loved these woods, maybe just for spite he'd sell the place to a foreign country for the building of a shoddy shopping mall that nobody wanted, with all signs in a foreign language, and just to spite Bert's boy who was known to love the place."

What a terrible thought! Then came another. What about those men who built the marina to replace his father's? If they smelled another profit and could buy the property, they likely wouldn't hesitate to bulldoze away sacred Indian grounds, sacred at least to StarWalker and me and all those Erie Indians they once saw dying in a terrible battle. Bud finally scolded himself for indulging in stupid conspiracy theories. We are to enjoy what we have when we have it.

He arrived at the clearing, this time not scaring one snake or squirrel on the way in. Maybe they and he finally had learned to anticipate life's problems and adapt more comfortably. He snuggled down against his favorite tree trunk—it was still there, although various branches looked dead now. It felt so solid against his back.

Dad was gone, but for Bud life was not, at least not yet. The future had to be found in the wake of death. Was that possible? There was no choice. It had to be. Bud had learned at least one thing. Stubborn unbelief is a cold and endless and apparently dead-end street. He'd now read much of the work of C. S. Lewis—SkyWalker had told him about this English author years ago. Another Englishman never mentioned by SkyWalker, a poet by the name of William Cowper, had also come to Bud's attention. Cowper had written things that later were set to music in churches, with a few of his pieces finding their way into literature books that Bud now used in his classrooms.

Sitting there against the tree on this crisp morning, Bud thought of Cowper, but could think of the exact words of only one simple verse he'd written. It bounced around in his mind and heart, helping those terrible ship images to fade into the background of his brain.

> Judge not the Lord by feeble sense,
> But trust Him for His grace;
> Behind a frowning providence
> He hides a smiling face.

Yesterday, Ed Sinclair and Herb Welch had surely helped a longstanding "frowning" to turn into a recognition of God's surprising and smiling face. First Jessica, and now Bud and Bert, and Herb, and shortly Maggie they hoped, had or would understand things more clearly and find rest in God, accepting forgiveness by God's grace, and do so despite the "feeble sense" that drives so much of our lives.

Bud found himself thinking about his own treasure chest, one in which he'd begun keeping his own secret collection of memory objects, and without at first having even looked carefully into his mother's little chest. In his was the furry tail of that little pest Lucky had caught when they first found Morning Glen and then met StarWalker. There was that quarter his mom had given him for the man he'd jokingly told her was crying in the park—he'd tricked her with the silly hot dog cry, but she'd given him the quarter anyway and he'd never spent it, keeping it to remember his mom's kindness in the midst of all her personal misery.

He, of course, also had kept the spoke from the stagecoach wheel that StarWalker had given him, presumably a leftover from the hidden city still under Lake Milton. Unfortunately, it wouldn't fit, so he kept it close by, pretending it was in the chest. He'd even wanted to put in a ball from the old park's bowling alley, but he never could get his hands on one of them—and it wouldn't have fit either. There also was his own much-read copy of that novel about Winesburg, Ohio, and now he'd add his dad's war medal. Despite what his dad had thought, it deserved a place of honor.

It was so easy to remember things when he was in Morning Glen, and such physical objects in his chest would help his memory when he was far from this village again. As soon as he got home and back to his chest, he'd write a note and put it inside. The note would say, "Turn the key, Son!" On behalf of Bert, he would sign it "Your loving dad." If he ever followed his dad's advice and risked loving some woman, that surely would be a big turning of the key! Maybe the day would come when his own son or daughter would open this chest and marvel at its contents—not sure what some of them even were.

He glanced up toward the sky, seeing at least little pieces of it through the highest branches. "How sad that most objects, when out of their original contexts, have no meaning at all to later generations. All generations pass along the paths of inevitable change. No matter. I am determined to keep my little chest anyway, and Mom's too."

Bud also thought about Betsy. Maybe the idea of his actually having a child of his own someday wasn't completely farfetched. On the other hand, in this clearing he'd seen visions that might have been delusions rather than reality. She could be another one of those. If so, how sad!

He could hardly have hoped for more during this refreshing visit, likely the last to his beloved Morning Glen. Then his attention was suddenly pulled from warm thoughts of Betsy and attracted to the opposite side of the clearing. Amazingly, he was standing there, silent at first, but nonetheless there, or he certainly seemed to be. StarWalker began to approach Bud, walking softly on the leaves with his flexible moccasins designed for stealth. There was no fear here, only mystery and anticipation.

When he got close enough, the old Indian's hand extended toward Bud in a beckoning gesture. There was nothing in it, no more objects for Bud's private treasure chest. StarWalker came right up to him and gently grasped his right hand, one hand with a splotchy red spot on it holding another with something similar. They were fellow travelers of the years, with each carrying the evidence of their difficulty.

"Hello, Bud. It's good to see you again! We have a little trip to take together. Just hold my hand and believe. I'll take care of the rest." A trip? StarWalker and Bud had never before left the clearing together to go anywhere. But Bud was in a trusting mood, so he took StarWalker's hand. Despite its obvious age, it was strong, even warm and tender.

They surely went somewhere, somehow from there, although exactly how Bud would never quite understand. Was this one of those "judge not by feeble sense" times? The mechanics of the trip apparently didn't matter. Bud felt lighter than air, not bound by gravity, free to go wherever and do whatever his friend and celestial guide had in mind. He filled with a warming thought. "How good it is to be guided by one greater than ourselves!"

StarWalker and Bud were now high in the air over Craig Beach, apparently going on a sightseeing tour of some kind. When Bud first dared to look down, as StarWalker instructed, he found himself looking at the little house on Beach Lane, the modest site of so many boyhood memories. The village seemed insignificant from above, a puzzle of mostly unassembled pieces aimlessly scattered along the lakeside.

"What do you see down there, Bud?"

"I see yesterday, happy, mostly sad though. I see my home that I'm now selling. It's an old house about to be a Jakas rental."

"Honor it as once yours, Bud, and then freely let it go. Let it be Mike's. Don't grasp too tightly what once was; that way you can more easily take hold of what might still be. Keep your hands open and free. Now that you've gone to the bank and emptied that box of your mom's, remember your dad's instruction, and be generous with yourself and others."

Next, having moved in seconds less than several hundred yards by ground distance, they were looking down on a little dark spot just behind the now closed amusement park. Bud quickly recognized that it was the mystery pond near Delores' house. It didn't look nearly as threatening from up here. It was a virtual nothing, a speck on a cluttered landscape, little more than a wet hole. If there ever was a dragon in that pond, you sure couldn't tell it from high above, and it might be so small that it couldn't scare a fly! Bud almost felt sorry for it, if it was even there, of course. It certainly had limited room to live and no way of escape, like so many others who had lived—or at least existed--in the village over the years.

"Is there a monster down in that speck of water, Bud?"

"I don't know, StarWalker, nobody does. Why are we looking at this? What should I do?"

"We are looking so that you can do what you must. You must release your many fears, Bud. Let them drop down into that watery darkness, and then just leave them there. It's better that they remain locked in mystery than be allowed to saddle you every day, and to no good end. Drop them now, drop them, Bud! Bomb that dragon with memories and fears that you're better off without. Dare to replace them with a little faith. Rather than rumors and doubts, begin to believe in what spans the years and survives bodily decay and death—and, believe me, there are such things!"

Bud squeezed his eyes closed and tried hard to do just that, figuring that the pond couldn't be hurt with a little more negative stuff that he didn't want anyway. "Leave me and let me live!"

Then StarWalker tugged at Bud's hand and his eyes came open. "Bud, we have only three more things to see. The first isn't far from the pond." Soon Bud realized that they were stopped high above a large roof on a building that he didn't remember being there. It wasn't far from the Catholic parish. Had the people built a giant new bingo hall?

"What's that building, StarWalker?"

"It's a new library for the area, only built three years ago. We're stopping here because of what it is and what you need to do."

"What do you mean?"

"You have written over the years about us, your life, your reflections, even your finally emerging faith. These memoirs potentially have meaning for others. Promise me that before you leave the area you will place the copy you have with you in that library. Since you grew up here, they will be glad to accept it as part of local history. Our stories are valuable and can be guides to others."

"I have written, StarWalker, that's true. It keeps my thoughts alive, at least for me. That's partly why I love literature—the thoughts of so many others survive and can become mine. As life's story unfolds, and is not forgotten but shared, wisdom seems to emerge. You can see the larger picture of things."

"Yes, Big Bud. Do you remember the stories I've told you about the Erie Indians, the Hutchins family from Connecticut, and Fredricksburg town, and more? Now you know many stories of your own, including the very important one Herb Welch just told you. Don't let these stories just die. Maybe now you can see why Christians and Jews before them value so much the stories of their "exodus" from Egypt, their captivity in Babylon, and finally the coming of their Messiah in a little town called Bethlehem. When these stories become your own, they change you!"

"Well, StarWalker, if you think this new library would want my writing and somebody would read it someday, I'll take it there, I promise, and I'll keep writing. You're encouraging me to think my journey is far from over, right?" StarWalker said nothing, only smiled as they sailed along in the velvet of the morning air.

Then came the next to last stop, not half a mile from the library. Even though they now were out over the open water of Lake Milton, Bud felt no fear. He was with a good friend who always seemed to have his best interest at heart and apparently knew even the invisible paths that crisscross among the distant skies. StarWalker obviously wanted Bud to look down at the lake, deep down below the surface. This water wasn't nearly as dark as the tiny pond. In fact, in places he could see all the way to the bottom. Fascinating!

What appeared down there frightened him at first. There were strange shapes that were arranged in patterns, like the foundations of very old houses now mostly rotted away. There were tracks here and there among the foundations, maybe abandoned streets that used to carry horses and stagecoaches. Nothing moved. Nothing was alive anymore, except a stray fish or two gliding about with no memory of life in a frontier town generations ago. Then Bud saw a big boot. Was it the same one he'd caught and thrown back? Whatever once had been alive down there had left its structural bones in a useless and abandoned array of slippery silence.

"What do you see, Bud?"

Bud strained his eyes and stretched his imagination. "I think it must be Fredericksburg that you told me about once. Wow!"

"That's right, it's the original home of your spoke. Now that you finally see it and know it was real, what does it mean to you?"

"Well, I've begun to think that what we build in this world is short-lived and very fragile—it makes a man think hard about what's really important in life. It makes me remember that writing of the poet Langston Hughes about the ancient rivers that gather the remnants of the years and just keep rolling along and carrying things away."

"Exactly, Bud, exactly! And let me tell you a very important thing. You need to meet people at their points of special need while they're still alive. Be a starwalker to them. You have the money from the bank. Use it well. *Be me to others!*"

That sounded to Bud like something that Pastor Ed Sinclair had said. Jesus is to be alive in us so that people meet him in what we say and do. It was Paul, he thought, who had said in his book to the Galatian believers, "It is no longer I who live, but it is Christ who lives in me." Star-Walker knew Bud's thought and said only, "Precisely! The verse is 2:20 if you want to check it later."

The next thing that Bud realized was that he could feel that strong tree trunk supporting his back again. The trip apparently was over as suddenly as it had begun. He opened his eyes, ready to talk more with Star-Walker about their amazing little adventure together, wanting to explore further the meanings his Indian friend was intending for him. He certainly wanted to thank him for those penetrating views of yesterday—which were really designed to be openings into tomorrow.

Bud glanced around the clearing. There was no StarWalker! He was gone. Had he ever been there? At least one thing was sure. Bud Kraemer was not alone anymore, not painfully alone as he had felt he was so many times before. Whether his eyes could see StarWalker or not, he knew he was not alone!

But StarWalker had said there would be one more scene, one more vision. He looked about and wondered if his friend had made a mistake. Then he noticed something nearby that he hadn't seen before. Over by another tree, just where StarWalker had been before their trip together, he now saw two of God's most lovely creatures. They were so delicate, so colorful and playful, so suggestive of life at its most innocent and best.

They were butterflies, Monarchs Bud thought, kings of true life not startled by his presence. They were just fluttering about and enjoying things, seeming to be there just for him. He watched them, wondering whether they had come—or been brought--as his final lesson. What a school nature can be! He thought about trying to capture one of them for his memory chest, but decided against it. Freedom was their nature, wasn't it, and of his nature also!

Eventually Bud managed to break his focus on the lovely scene of the dancing butterflies. Apparently his visit in the clearing was now over. It well could be his last ever. The available time had gone, his personal agendas were more than met, and another matter and place now called. Bud slowly stood, feeling the full height of his stature, higher without all the fears, straighter without having to know all the answers, released from so many yesterdays, now beckoned forward by some new tomorrows that twinkled with unusually bright light.

In Morning Glen, as always, Bud Kraemer had found—or been *given*—the vision of a new day and the graciousness of a special presence from beyond himself. With that presence, insight, faith, and hope filling him, he hurried back to his car. There was a new excitement in his steps. It was almost like his dog Lucky was with him again, playfully, even if accidentally showing him Morning Glen for the first time. Well, that was yesterday. This was today, a really good new day. Betsy was waiting for him—*and so was life*!!

www.ingramcontent.com/pod-product-compliance
Lightning Source LLC
Chambersburg PA
CBHW060402030726
47497CB00003B/822